Fallen Love

William Price Jr

To Jacky Dumas, for first introducing me to gothic storytelling.

And to Tom Paine, for teaching me that the greatest truths are in fiction.

1

    dam pushed his glass forward again, and Candace refilled it.

Like all her regulars, scattered around their usual spots on worn barstools and stained booths, he seemed to ignore the world lying beyond the large, cloudy window that read, "Waystation." Unlike her other regulars, he never made a grab for her, no matter how far down the bottle he went. Adam never made comments on her large chest, nor how time was starting to take its toll. Some days, Candace felt even older than this decrepit bar, both of them sagging and tired, both of them carrying the weight of too many years spent with too many drunks. Despite the press of time, and despite the odd remark made at her expense by one of the Waystation's usual losers, Candice always felt the years ease around Adam. Her ass was safe around him, regardless of the tight jeans she had to wear in search of tips. Hell, she could even take off the stupid ball cap the owner made her wear and air out her long auburn hair in the weak breeze of the creaking overhead fans. She could do this without having to worry about Adam making some smart-ass remark about the few grays starting to appear.

Not that Adam spoke much anyway. In fact, in the few months he had been coming to the Waystation, Candace could not remember him saying more than a dozen words to anyone. Even getting his name had taken the better part of three weeks. He only communicated with the occasional asshole who got too forward with her, and then only with a look through long, disheveled hair that warned of violence. His soft, sunken eyes, rarely leaving the glass Candice always placed in front of him, spoke of some deep pain, but one he would not share.

Every now and then Candace would try to get something out of him. "In the mood for anythin' different tonight?" she sometimes asked.

"Same's fine," he always replied in a hollow, yet somehow gentle voice, pushing his glass forward once more.

She would then refill his glass. "I can get you somethin' harder." Candice would then nod towards the row of bottles behind her, gratefully obscuring the large mirror that ran the length of the bar and its unwelcome reflections. "We've all kinds of sin here, you know."

He would just throw back his drink and push the glass forward again.

Candace would then sigh, accepting the futility of the conversation. "Is there anythin' else I can do for you?" she would ask, sometimes suggestively leaning forward, sometimes not.

"You're fine like this."

And so, tonight, instead of a futile conversation or an even more futile flirtation, Candace just nodded, refilling Adam's drink and the pretzel bowl at his elbow before moving down to the other end of the weathered bar. Less than an hour ago, a teenaged girl had come in with a boy only a little older than herself, and Candace had been trying to keep an eye on them. Her first instinct had been to throw both kids out, but they had proper I.D., or the fakes were good enough anyway, and her boss had made clear that she was not to turn away a paying customer.

Within a half-hour of their coming in, though, Candace's instincts had looked to be right. Glancing at the young lovers, she had to fight the urge to cuss. Since they had started drinking, his behavior had gone from bad to you-need-to-get-your-ass-to-church. Every time Candace glanced over, the little bastard was doing everything he could to seduce the sad-looking girl. The poor thing was obviously fighting back tears, barely listening to whatever nonsense the little snake was hissing in her ear. Candace could not tell if she was naturally this pale, or if something had happened to drain away what little color the girl had. Something was obviously bothering her, and all the appletinis he kept ordering and she kept throwing back were obviously doing little to still the tremble in her hands.

Ignoring all her better instincts, Candace tried derailing the oncoming tragedy. "How you kids doin'?" she asked the children.

The girl blinked her big black eyes though her long, black bangs. Unshed tears swam within those bloodshot pools, more evidence of the bad times this girl must have only recently seen. She buried her face in her hands. "I think I might pass out."

"You won't pass out," the snake assured her. "You're doing just fine."

She reached out and downed another drink, bringing another slithery smile to the face of her seducer.

"We're doing just fine barmaid." The snake reached a manicured hand into the back pocket of his designer jeans and pulled out his wallet. He made little effort concealing a wad of bills. From this, he pulled out a twenty and laid it on the bar. "Why don't you set us up again?" he said to Candace in a tone that was entirely dismissive.

The girl pulled her face up, revealing smears of dark makeup. "Shots," she sighed. "I need shots."

Her reptilian companion smiled coldly at the girl. "You heard the lady, a round of shots."

Candace grimaced, but took the cash and poured them a round. Unable to resolve the conflict between trying to help and fearing the consequences, she left the couple to their business. From the corner of her eye, however, Candace noticed the young gentleman slipping a little something extra into his companion's drink.

Tending to her work, Candice considered her options. She feared trying to interfere again with a man taking advantage of a girl, her hand unconsciously going to the small scar her v-neck t-shirt concealed. The cops would take too long to respond, if they came at all. The handful of regulars had wandered out over the past hour, to drift home or just pass out in a ditch. All, that is, but one.

"Somethin' bad's gonna happen," Candace said, pouring Adam another drink.

"Something always does."

"Sometimes *somethin'* can be prevented." She reached out with a soft touch and raised his face. They locked eyes before Candace looked meaningfully to the far end of the bar.

Adam followed her gaze but immediately looked back to his glass, shaking off Candace's touch. "Not my problem."

"It's someone's problem."

"Let *someone* deal with it."

Without warning, the little girl stood and, no longer holding her tears, began to make her swaying way towards the door, bringing her in Adam's direction. Her boyfriend was chivalrous enough to slither up and help steady her, though his kindness was marred by the hand on her skinny ass.

"You know what he's doin'," Candace urgently whispered.

"Her fault," Adam replied, keeping his eyes fixed down. He finished his drink and pushed the glass forward. "Her consequences."

Candace crossed her arms. "*Your* decision not to help."

The happy couple lost their footing and bumped into the bar very close to Adam. The unwelcome jolt knocked over his glass and caused a muscle in his cheek to twitch.

The snake laughed at the minor mishap, pulling his next meal back to her feet. "Sorry, friend," he said, patting Adam on the shoulder before slithering to the door.

Candace saw that Adam's face had gone utterly blank. She leaned in. "Please help her," she breathed.

"Dammit," he growled through clenched teeth, standing.

Adam walked outside the Waystation, unsurprised that the happy couple had only managed to get a short distance. The unlit, garbage-strewn street was empty but for what had to be Slick's car, as it was the nicest thing in this, the shittiest part of town. It was also the only car on the street, all other predators having already retreated from the coming dawn; all but one. The concrete river was silent and dark, without a single light from the surrounding businesses, either those boarded up or those still struggling to survive. The faint light from the open door of Slick's sports car cast a pale line against the deep, pre-dawn darkness, pointing straight at the approaching Adam.

As he moved closer, Adam noticed the little scumbag was trying to keep his grip on the nearly catatonic girl in his arms while struggling with his keys and the car door. "Hey asshole," Adam called out flatly.

Slick half turned, dropping the girl into the street like so much dead weight, and reached for what Adam sort of hoped was a weapon. "Don't try anything stupid here, friend," the boy said in a squeaking voice.

Adam stopped and took a deep breath. "Ok, two things. One: I'm not your friend, so stop calling me that; it's pissing me off. Two:

step away from the girl, go home, jerk off, and forget you ever met her."

"Or what?"

"Or I'll to *try* not to kill you, but I won't try very hard."

"Fuck you!" Slick tried to reach under his untucked shirt. Adam shot forward, only an instant behind his thrown blade. His knife caught Slick in the hand just as the man himself caught the boy by the throat. Adam was already pummeling Slick in the face and gut even before the small gun the boy had tried to draw fell uselessly to the street. There was no real need for the beating, the knife in the boy's hand having effectively ended the fight, but Adam had some things he needed to work through.

Besides, this little shit obliviously needs an ass-kicking.

After beating the young stud's face into his spiffy car a few times, idly wondering if it was insured, Adam remembered to retrieve his blade. Grabbing the knife, still imbedded in Slick's hand, Adam pulled up and out, splitting the hand into two halves. For good measure he also broke the little bastard's jaw and stomped on his tiny balls a few times.

Once Slick was nice and unconscious, Adam took a few deep breaths, letting the flames out and slowing his thundering heart. He reached into the side pocket of his white leather coat and pulled out a small cigar, then lit it and pulled a long drag. A moan drew his attention back to the girl still lying in the street.

"Ah, shit." Adam glanced at the Waystation, but Candace was hanging the CLOSED sign with a shrug and a smile.

Desperately, Adam looked up and down the deserted road but saw nothing.

"Are we still getting out of here?" the drugged girl moaned before starting to snore.

"DAMMIT!"

2

$\mathcal{H}$olly woke to her own, personal Hell. A pair of pliers were attached to her head and someone was squeezing down hard. Her mouth tasted like something had dirty sex in it… without lube. Her tongue felt like someone else had puked down her throat. Every time she tried to breathe, some of that sex/puke/death came up and out through her nostrils. Her whole universe was the pain and the… ugh. If she could, she would have just laid down wherever she was forever… but her rotten stomach decided otherwise.

As she was throwing up, Holly became increasingly convinced she was in Hell. It was hot as balls, but she was shivering. The lights were way too bright, making her feel like some dickhead cop was shining his flashlight in her face. She had no idea how she got here, but she kinda had the feeling she deserved being... wherever. And, oh yeah, Holly was throwing up so hard, she was pretty sure her eyes were going to pop out. She was in Hell. Or maybe Dallas.

"WHENEVER YOU'RE DONE!!!!!"

"Oww!" Holly protested. Whoever that miserable bastard was with the impossibly loud voice, he really needed to shut up. "Quiet," she whispered with a finger to her lips. "Quiet good. Talking bad." Holly tried to cover the evil sunlight with her eyes but it just seemed to be everywhere.

A source of wonderful coolness was put against her hand. It was solid and round and stable, unlike the rest of the spinning world. Her angel, her amazing benefactor and protector, had brought her a glass of ice water. Holly's throat screamed at her with a fiery hatred, but somehow, this wonderful angel had known of her need and delivered to her the remedy. She brought the perfect coolness to her tiny mouth and reveled in the feeling of icy relief.

"Not too fast," her angel warned in a deep, soft voice. "You'll just puke it up again."

The water of life greatly eased her suffering, so Holly felt brave enough to try to open her eyes again. Still the damned light was just too painful. This time, however, she spotted another source of relief. She reached down to the stained coffee table in front of her and grabbed, after a few tries, the large sunglasses lying upon it. Once safely covering here burning eyes, Holly was able to view her surroundings with only minor agony.

Hell has a really shitty decorator.

Holly was sitting on a ratty old couch in the corner of some dingy, one-bedroom apartment. The nasty green carpet had several holes in it, not to mention a fresh pile of vomit. The curtain rod was missing curtains, which was unfortunate since the view out the small window was only to the window of the next apartment, and Holly idly thought that meth lab might like a little privacy. The kitchen cubicle showed no signs of use, other than the dead rat and colony of ants that were working on it. Somewhere in the distance, Holly could hear a car going by; either a car or just some vibrating metal, anyway.

"Nice place," she said, leaning her head back against the couch and hoping she wouldn't stick to it.

"Thanks." Her benefactor, a medium sized guy with a thick build, took the glass and put it down on the stained coffee table.

He wasn't a bad looking guy. Or at least, he wouldn't be if he took a shower and practiced a little grooming, you know, once a century. Not to mention his sense of fashion was shit. Who the hell wears a long-sleeved shirt in the middle of a Texas summer?

"Feeling better?" he asked, without much interest.

Holly rubbed her head and nodded. "A little," she replied.

"Good, now get out." He jerked his head towards the door.

"What happened last night?" Holly asked. She looked around at the guy's apartment with a sinking feeling. "Oh God, we didn't..."

"No," he replied flatly. "Your boyfriend slipped you something. Get out." Another motion towards the door.

Holly carefully leaned forward, picking up the glass of water for another sip. "He's *soo* not my boyfriend," she insisted. "He just said he could help me out."

"Didn't ask. Don't care. Get out."

The girl put her glass down and rubbed her arms, still shivering a bit despite the midsummer heat. Although great for clubbing, the black leather skirt and satin blouse she had worn out the night before really didn't do much for comfort during the day.

Then the memories of last night began piling in, pressing against her mind, and reaching their taloned-fingers around her quickening heart. Coming home… her parents… the blood… everywhere. The thought and memories filled her eyes. Another flood of sorrow and regret. Images and horrors adding even more pain and misery to her already-suffering soul. Holly had been dancing and flirting and hating her parents while they were being…

God, I'd give anything for some shorts and a comfy t-shirt right now.

Holly almost desperately looked around for some way to divert her train of thought. "Do you have any crackers or anything?" she asked.

"I've got vomit, nice and fresh. Feel free to take some on your way out."

"Yeah..." Holly slowly pulled the sunglasses off and looked at the door. "I don't actually have anywhere to go," she admitted, forcing down the reality of last night to face the reality of today. She turned her wide-eyed, well-practiced gaze to him. "Is there any way that I could...?"

"No," he replied, cutting off her plea before she could even finish it. The hulking man leaned forward and put a finger onto the girl's forehead. "Look princess, I figure you're used to opening those big, dark eyes and having the boys fall all over themselves to make you happy, but that ain't happening here. Let me make a few things very clear." He jabbed a thumb into his chest. "I saved your narrow ass last night, against my better judgment, because I was guilted into it." He poked the tip of his finger in her chest. "I don't know you, I don't like you, and I don't want to do either." He stood up straight and pointed towards the door. "Now. Get. Out."

"Where am I supposed to go?" she demanded with tears in her eyes.

"I don't care. Go home. Tell your parents they were right about everything and agree to whatever..."

"My parents are dead, asshole!" Holly jumped to her feet, her sudden rage overriding her sorrow and hangover. "I'd love to go back and tell them they were right but they're dead!"

She had to take several deep breaths, struggling against a tide that would drag her down and never let her come up again. "And everything I own in the world is in a small bag at the bus station!" Holly stormed towards the door. "I spent all night partying with my friends- we were free at last! Only my folks were getting murdered while I was… while I was out… FUCK YOU!!!" Holly grabbed the door, ready to put this latest of a long line of assholes behind her.

"Wait," he said in a flat voice.

"No," she snapped, standing at the door. "To Hell with you, to Hell with your attitude, and to Hell with your crappy apartment."

"Who's trying to kill you?" he asked with very little enthusiasm.

"I thought you didn't care."

He directed a look that spoke volumes about his lack of caring. "You've got three seconds before I slam the door in your face."

Holly used two of the seconds before closing the door and returning to the couch. "Can I at least ask your name?" she asked after taking another sip of water.

He paused a second. "Adam," he finally said. He sighed and walked to the opposite wall, leaning against it, and crossing his arms over his broad chest. "Dammit," he grumbled under his breath. "Now who's trying to kill you? Who killed your parents?"

Holly could not help but hug herself tightly, huddling against the memory of finding her house surrounded by sirens and reporters. The memory of two body bags being carried out. "I don't know who they are. My dad had some kind of business with them."

"Drugs?" Adam guessed. "Guns?"

Holly shook her head. "No, I think he just got them some trucks. My dad worked for Agarés, on Fort Burleson. They paid him to get a bunch of Army trucks from the company."

"And after he did, they came for him." It was not a question.

Holly could only shrug a tiny shrug, the weight of everything continuing to press down on her. "The cops showed up and took me to the police station."

Adam rubbed the back of his neck. "Is there anything you can tell me about them? About the people who killed your parents." he asked. "Did you see anyone? Hear anything? Why do you think they're still coming after you?"

Holly took a few moments to compose herself, during which Adam just stood waiting. Finally, she took a deep breath and continued. "The cops said it was a break-in. The house was trashed.

While I was sitting in some lieutenant's office, another cop gave me coffee to drink, then nothing. I woke up in a warehouse or something. It was dark. I was handcuffed and I heard chanting. I got free and ran."

"Wait," Adam interrupted. "How did you get out of the restraints?"

"My uncle taught me a trick for getting out of cuffs."

"Cop?"

"Magician." She smiled sadly at the memory. "He thought so, at least."

"What about Slick?" Adam asked.

"Slick?"

"The guy from last night. At the bar."

"That was Reese. I knew him from school, but he graduated last year. He's a rich kid, kinda spoiled, but ok... I thought he was ok. After... when I ran away, I went back to the club to try and find some friends, and Reese was there. He offered to help, said he could get me out of Meropis County, but he had to wait for his mom to make some arrangements. We were... we were only supposed to wait at that bar for a little while, but he offered to buy me a drink to help... to feel..."

Holly took a deep, shuttering breath. "That's the last thing I remember. Going into the bar with Reese. Then here."

Holly had something else to say but hesitated, fearing her story was already moving past any hint of believability. Adam just sighed and rolled a hand in the air. "Out with it," he commanded. "If I haven't called bullshit at the chanting, I think I'm ready for anything."

"No, you're not," Holly warned. "Four people were in another part of the warehouse, standing around some kind of altar. They were all wearing robes and they were the ones chanting."

Adam said nothing. There was no sign on his weathered face if he believed the outlandish story. "Anything else?" he asked.

Holly nodded. "On the altar were chains and some animal and... blood. The blood had been used to paint symbols."

"What symbols?"

"I don't know, weird ones. Like writing."

"Describe it."

"Hard," she said. "All straight lines. Every corner had little stars on them."

Adam started at the description. He stared at her with a strange expression, like regret mixed with anger mixed with... something else. Just as Holly was growing uncomfortable, starting to think up some explanation, some story that would make him believe her incredible story, Adam turned. He moved to the counter of the kitchen cubicle, absently kicking aside the dead rat with his bare foot, and picked up a pad and pencil. He sketched something and then handed the pad over to Holly. The girl looked down at the symbols he had effortlessly drawn and stared in open-mouthed shock.

She looked back up and held the pad up to him in accusation, pointing a finger at the symbols.

"How the hell do you know about these?" she demanded. "What are these?"

"Proof you're not full of shit," he replied.

He returned to the kitchen, retrieving a fifthly plastic cup and filling it with faucet-water. Adam muttered something beneath his breath before drinking. A deep sigh followed, with a rough hand pulling through his disheveled hair.

"What?" Holly asked.

He sighed again. "Just... memories. Bad ones, mostly." Adam glanced up to the ceiling, as though he was looking at something or someone above, and shook his head. "I guess I should have figured they wouldn't leave me alone. Wouldn't let me just... go."

Adam straightened then, standing his full height and squaring his shoulders. He turned and moved purposefully into the bedroom. "I don't know how," he called out through the open door. "But your family managed to get the attention of some people who need to be dealt with."

Holly stood and looked into the bedroom, gasping in shock. Adam had pulled some slightly less filthy clothes from a pile in the closet. The man had removed his shirt, exposing his upper body. His entire torso, his chest, back, stomach, everything, was covered in tattoos. The markings were identical to the writing she had seen on the altar around which her kidnappers had been standing.

"You're one of them," she said, backing away in sudden terror.

Adam froze as he had been reaching for the fresher clothes. "No," he grimaced.

"Bullshit!" she snapped.

He half-turned towards her with a flat look on his deeply creased face. "I'm not," he repeated. "These are… different than what you saw before."

She shook her head. "You expect me to believe…"

Adam sat on the edge of his bed. He glanced down at the marks, which trailed down his arms. "The writing you saw before was… it was part of a ritual. They're worshipping something. Something… dark. I've had experience with these kinds of things. Hence, the marks."

The girl shook her head slightly.

"Look, you can either believe I saved you from Slick last night just to take you back to that cult, or you can believe what I'm telling you." He looked up at her, remaining seated on the unmade bed. "Nothing I say will likely convince you; you have to decide. Slick screwed you over, probably just for the chance to mount you, and that's got you scared. Scared is good; scared is careful. But scared can also keep you from taking help when it's offered.

"It's a hell of a coincidence," Holly noted, "you just happening to know about these…"

"There are no coincidences," Adam replied, almost automatically. "But there is free will, free choice. Either way, make yours."

Holly hesitantly stepped forward, standing over the unmoving Adam, and tracing a light finger on one of the patches of writing inscribed on his thick shoulder. The large man did not move or react much at all to her light touch, except to look away, almost in shame. "What kind of experience?" she asked softly.

"What?"

"You said you had experience with things like this. What kind of experience?"

"The bad kind," he grumbled, is sunken eyes still fixed on the far wall. Finally, Adam stood, forcing Holly to take a half-step back but still only a hair's breadth apart, and looked down at her. "I've seen what these kinds of people do," he said in a hard voice that seemed somehow to push against and through her. He turned back to the closet. "They need to be dealt with."

Abruptly, he unbuckled his pants and made as though to let them drop. Holly started spun, exiting the bedroom, her heart and burning ears making her suddenly aware of which room she had been standing in.

"You're right that they're trying to kill you," Adam continued from the bedroom as Holly returned to the living room, sounding like he was rummaging through his clothes. "So until I get this sorted out, you need to stay here. If you try to leave, even just to leave town, they'll likely grab you before your make five blocks." Adam then also returned to the main room, pulling a new long-sleeved shirt over his head and looking for his boots.

"Do you know who they are?" she asked.

"Not really; or not specifically. It doesn't matter; one cult's the same as another."

"What do they want?"

"You don't want me to answer that."

"Well, what am I supposed to do while you're off doing... whatever?" Holly demanded.

"Don't know; don't care."

"Well... is there at least something to eat in this dump?"

Adam looked around and grimaced. He moved to the counter over which was thrown his white leather coat and pulled a large roll of cash from the pocket. Negligently tossing it at his unwanted guest, Adam grunted "Order a pizza."

Holly caught the thick roll of large-denomination bills with surprise. "How much is here?"

"I dunno."

She started counting but stopped at a thousand. "If you have money like this, why the hell do you live in this pit?" she demanded.

Adam threw on his white leather coat. "It suits me," he replied.

"How can you wear that thing? It's, like, a million degrees outside."

Adam sighed, rubbing his eyes. "I'm trying to climatize."

"To where? Hell?"

"Ok," he said, turning to face her. "Let's set a few ground rules. One: I hate conversation. Two: shut up. Three: I'm going to go take care of these people who are trying to kill you so you can leave as soon as possible. Four: shut up again. Five: don't go anywhere. Questions?"

"Why can't I go with you?"

"Because you're annoying," he calmly replied. "Not to mention you've got people who are TRYING. TO. KILL. YOU."

"But I don't want to be stuck here," she pouted. In the back of her mind, Holly was calculating how far she could get with the large roll of bills.

"Fine." Adam opened the door and gestured outside. "Go. Take that cash and go wherever you want. Disanté is great. There's plenty to do in this town. I'll send flowers to your funeral. It's your choice; stay and live, or go and die."

Without another word, Adam walked out the door, leaving it open for Holly to make her decision.

3

The ugliness of Disanté was all the more obvious in the first hours of day, absent the distracting camouflage of busy humans. Crumpled remains of discarded people lie in this alley and that, glancing timidly at and flinching away from the few passers-by. The garish smears of half-decayed carcasses lie where whatever vehicle or mob of near-feral children had crushed them. Insects joyously flittered from meat to meat, living or dead, as they basked in the already-sweltering heat of the midsummer day. Old buildings crumbled away alongside new construction in a parody of community continuity. Disanté was a city consuming itself and those condemned to live within.

These things only peripherally registered in Adam's mind as he made his way through the concrete oven to his objective. He had long-since resigned himself to Hell, after all; why bother focusing on how similar Earth was becoming to his ultimate destination? Instead, Adam just focused his mind on his current task, his current goal. He only ever glanced up from his path once he came in sight of his destination, letting his body make its own way.

He entered the sandwich shop with only a brief, silent acknowledgement of the drop in temperature. Any business that wanted to stay in business paid a premium for its air conditioning in an almost futile battle against the Texas midsummer. Adam sat down at the far end of the large counter, positioning himself to have a view of the many booths and tables, the kitchen door tucked back with the bathrooms and janitorial closet. When the waitress arrived, Adam quickly ordered himself breakfast to save her from the litany the already tired-looking woman was forced to spew at every new customer. He then absently thanked her, communicating his desire for solitude, and patiently waited. The shop was nearly empty now, being in one of those strange lulls between early morning laborers and late morning professionals, but Adam was confident his prey would arrive in time.

He glanced occasionally out of the café's large, wraparound windows towards the surprisingly modern police department building across the street. Considering how old and run-down most of Disanté looked, the headquarters of its peace officers was a sharp contrast to the city's otherwise oppressive urban decay. A black marble sign in front read: "Disanté Police. To Protect…" Idly curious, Adam had asked someone not long after his arrival about the sign and why it was missing part of the traditional motto; he was given two answers, both he believed. First, the city had run out of money and could not afford to finish the sign after spending so much on the jail, riot equipment, tactical vehicles, and other tools of population control. Second, some members of Disanté's local government had suffered a momentary combination of political honesty and social satire, betraying the true purpose of this force; these police only protected, and then only the interests of Disanté's wealthy. With all this in mind, Adam ate his grease-dripping breakfast and waited for the one person left whom he could almost call a friend.

His patience received its reward in so little time, even he was a little surprised. Not long after Adam's arrival, a steady stream of cops had begun filtering in, most in search of cheap coffee. Most took their orders and left, but some sat down for a brief relief from the day's worsening heat before venturing out to enforce Man's law onto the populace. Thus, there were more than a few occupied booths when Sergeant Isandro walked in. Adam had, in fact, only barely finished his semi-fluid omelet when he saw the familiar face pass through the front door.

Patience always wins out.

Sergeant Isandro was a good cop and a good man. Tall and lean, he wore his uniform like a second skin, showing no discomfort at the weight of his gun belt nor the morning's rising heat. Although his heritage was clearly of this land or nearby, Isandro spoke with little or no accent, except when speaking Spanish, which he did flawlessly. The few times Adam had seen the good cop since their first encounter, Isandro had always acted professionally, treating all those with whom he interacted respectfully, but firmly, in his capacity as a peace officer.

I hope he doesn't make me have to kick his ass.

Isandro walked up to the counter and called out to the waitress who had been chatting with the briefly-idle cook. "Hey, *Maríposa*! *¿Cómo estás?*"

The matronly brunette smiled and blew him a kiss. "*Hola, Enriqué.*" She motioned for him to sit on one of the cushioned stools lining the counter as she wrote up his usual order.

Adam slipped up behind the good cop and sat down beside him without drawing the man's attention. "How have you been, Isandro?"

The good cop started and turned, his hand moving with lightning speed to his weapon. Seeing Adam, dressed as always in his white leather coat in spite of the heat, Isandro shook his head and returned to his appreciation of the waitress' figure. He did not, however, take his hand off his weapon. "Son of a bitch," he grumbled beneath his breath, loud enough that only Adam could hear.

"How would you know? You never met my mother."

"I don't think you even had a mother, *cabrón.*"

"Is that any way to talk to a friend?"

"Friend?" Isandro looked around the café before leaning in, one hand on the counter and the other still on his gun. "I could shoot you right here and have no problems at confession."

"True," Adam admitted. He reached over and slid his plate to continue breakfast. "Might have a problem with Internal Affairs, though."

The good cop laughed. "Somebody like you *must* have warrants out."

"Wouldn't surprise me."

"What the hell do you want, anyway?"

"Favor."

Isandro started laughing. He turned and fell back into a counter chair, struggling to regain his balance. Adam just continued to chew on a piece of undercooked sausage, smiling reassuringly at the waitress' curious look.

When the laughing fit finally passed and the good cop regained his breath, he wiped away his tears and looked at Adam. "You must be the dumbest man on Earth. I should actually thank you, you know. I used to think I was a bad Catholic until I met you." A few of the cops within the café had glanced curiously at Isandro's laughter, but the good cop waved off their gaze.

"Haven't heard of the Crusades?"

Isandro leaned in towards Adam. "Listen to me, *cabrón*," he muttered. "The only reason I don't arrest your ass right now is because I'm waiting for my coffee."

Adam looked right into Isandro's eyes. "You owe me."

"I owe you shit!" the good cop hissed. "You used up your first, last, and only favor that night!"

"You mean that night when I saved your life?" Adam asked calmly, returning to his meal.

"I mean that night that I had to…"

Adam calmly ate a piece of burnt toast. "Say it," he said through his food. "Say it… *officer*. That night you had to…?"

"That night I had to help you get rid of a body," Isandro finished in a hoarse whisper.

Adam nodded. "The body of a man who was trying to kill you." Adam turned back and stared hard into the good cop's eyes. "A man who *would* have killed you, slow, painful, if I hadn't saved your ass."

Isandro tried to hold the gaze but had to look away. "Bastard," he finally whispered.

"Never pretended to be anything else," Adam replied, finishing his water-thin orange juice.

"Do you have any idea how much that night…?" the good cop shook his head.

"Try drinking."

"What do you want?"

"A few nights ago, there was a break-in and double murder. Victims were named MacAllister. I need the report."

"What's your interest?"

"Give me your word that what I tell you goes no further."

"What's my word to you?"

Adam just waited.

The good cop sighed and shook his head. "Fine, *cabrón*. I swear it."

"I'm helping the daughter."

Isandro started. "*You've* got Holly MacAllister!" he hissed.

"Say it a little louder," Adam muttered. "I don't think the cook heard you."

"Asshole," the good cop hissed, "the whole damned department's been briefed on her. We've all been told to keep a look out."

"Yeah, that have anything to do with her getting drugged and kidnapped right out of your damned station?"

"What are you talking about?"

"Do you need it in Spanish? That girl was drugged and taken out of that building right across the street. The one with 'Police' written on it?"

"There's no way," Isandro firmly insisted. "Kidnappers don't get into a police station."

"Not unless they've got badges."

"Do you know what you're saying?"

"Yeah," Adam replied. "I'm saying get me that file so I can try and figure out the who, what, where, when, and how, before this girl ends up like her parents."

Isandro shook his head. The waitress arrived and wordlessly handed over a bag and cup. Her eyes said clearly that she sensed the tension between her pair of customers but, as a true professional, knew to mind her own business. She only spared a glance at Isandro, seeking reassurance from the peace officer. The good cop nodded confidence to her and, taking the items, he stood. "Wait here." He paused before leaving, and glanced back at Adam. "I can't believe you kept that guy's fucking coat," he muttered before walking out.

Adam looked down at the heavy white leather draped over his thick body. "It's a good coat," he shrugged.

Adam was on the final bites of his pie by the time Isandro returned. Luckily, he knew how to make his desserts last, so the sergeant had plenty of time to retrieve the file. Upon entering, Isandro jerked his head towards a corner booth, furthest from the few remaining police-customers. Adam stood and followed, bringing with him his sweating glass of milk.

"What have you got?"

Isandro slid the file across. "Other than some pretty lazy cop work, not much."

Adam glanced up as he took the file. "What do you mean?"

"No crime scene, no investigation, no witness statements, and the most half-assed autopsy I've ever heard of."

Adam started skimming through the file, reading the relevant parts. "Blunt-force trauma to the heads?"

"Yeah," Isandro confirmed. "That's your cause of death for both vics but it doesn't explain the mutilation."

"How bad?"

The good cop shook his head. "You usually only see it this bad on sexual assaults, cult activity, drug rampages, or animal attacks. Whoever attacked them cut off their hands and feet, and so disfigured their faces that they couldn't be identified."

"Then how do we know it's them?" Adam asked, taking a drink from his dripping cup.

"You mean besides matching body type, blood type, gender, and the fact that they were found in their own house?" The good cop leaned back in the cushioned booth and shrugged. "You're right, it could be anybody."

"Theory of the crime?" Adam asked, glancing through the handful of family photographs. One of Holly at her recent graduation, wearing the cap and gown of an honor graduate and proudly beaming. One of the girl standing with her father, hugging tightly. One of Holly and her mother, standing together.

"That's where the investigating officer really got lazy. A break-in that went bad." Isandro snorted while signaling the waitress for a glass of iced tea. "My ass. If it was a break-in that went sour, sure kill the parents, but take the time to mutilate them like that? No way. Plus, there was nothing missing."

"What's *your* take?"

"Personal." Isandro leaned back in and jabbed a finger towards the report. "Anytime there's that much attention, especially to the faces, it's personal. Whoever did it knew those two and really hated them. Honestly, if I was investigating, I'd look at the daughter."

"What about the kidnapping?"

"*If* it's true," the good cop retorted. The waitress brought Isandro's tea, laying the large dipping glass onto several napkins before leaving again. "Then that just confirms the crime being personal. Somebody is targeting that family."

Adam closed the file and leaned back. "Damn," he muttered. "Is there anything weird going on?" he suddenly asked.

"Define weird."

"Unsolved crimes. Open investigations that don't make logical sense."

"You just described ninety percent of what happens in this town."

"Come on, give me something."

"There really isn't anything. Petty theft has gone down, but random violence is up. There have been a few more kidnappings than usual but no bodies. That new biker gang that rolled into town last year but moved on? Word is they're on their way back."

"The Furies?"

Isandro nodded. "But like I said, they're somewhere on the south end of Austin right now, so I doubt there's a connection."

"You said your entire department was briefed on the MacAllister girl," Adam noted, raising his half-empty glass of milk and looking at Isandro across the rim. "Is that normal?"

"The case made the news. Whenever that happens, we usually get a heads-up. But now that you mention it, the briefing was a little more intense."

"How so?"

The good cop shook his head slightly, moving the ice in his glass with a straw. "Hard to say exactly. The Lieutenant wasn't acting weird, just... stressed. He usually only gets that way when there's pressure coming down from above."

"Political pressure?" Adam guessed.

Isandro stood, taking the file back. "Look, either way, it might be best if the girl just left town.

"Not yet."

"Well, whatever you're into, keep me out of it. If you're trying to do right by this girl, then God bless." The good cop raised his glass of tea in salute and drained it in one long pull. He then put down the empty glass and looked at Adam with serious eyes. "But you seem like the kind of person that trouble finds, and I'd rather not be around when it does." He stood and paused, giving Adam a meaningful look. "Again."

With that, Sergeant Isandro left.

Alone with his pie, Adam considered what he had learned and what his next step would be. A few options ran through his dark mind, and he dismissed each as unproductive. At last, he settled on a simple idea: he had asked a good cop, now he should ask a bad crook.

4

$\mathscr{S}$itting in the Waystation night after night, Adam could not help but overhear laid off workers and bankrupted small business owners bemoan the collapse of Seventh Avenue. In recent years, since the Agarés corporation had convinced the Texas State Legislature to build a new highway through town, businesses in Disanté had been gradually moving away from the traditional downtown and towards the completed freeway; this movement had the effect of diverting local money away from competitors and towards the new Agarés shopping center and other ventures. With the gradual migration of businesses, the old buildings had grown increasingly run down. What had been an, if not thriving, at least stable business district, was now little more than a demilitarized zone. Boarded up windows looked out on empty roads only sporadically lit by burned-out streetlights. Empty parking lots filled with trash and gang graffiti decorated the countless "closed-for-business" signs. The only indicators of life were the criminals and the police who ignored them.

Seventh Avenue used to be the center of Disanté. All the recreational activities in town had once been located there. The theater, shopping center, a few restaurants, and church were all once found along Seventh Avenue. Even the local government had been located there, both City Hall and the old police station. People once believed that Disanté's heart beat within Seventh Avenue.

Now it was rotten. You could still find entertainment there, but it was the kind that went along with the festering squalor of urban decay. A shining example of humanity's capacity for righteous indifference to itself. Drugs, prostitution, and every other shade of disorganized crime centered itself along Seventh Avenue. People still came here, but they did so quickly, seeking their specific sins, and usually leaving as soon as possible. In search of information, Adam entered this festering shrine to human abuse.

He did not seek a sin within Seventh Avenue, but a sinner. Not long after his arrival in Disanté, Adam had encountered a rather pathetic excuse of a criminal named Juan. Although he could not, at the time, imagine a situation in which he would ever willing seek out the minimally-successful miscreant, Adam nonetheless had made a mental note of Juan's typical location.

You never know when you might need a rat, after all.

The search was not a long one. At the corner of Seventh and J Street, Adam spotted him. The sun was still mid-climb, and the little bastard was already harassing a group of prostitutes, ordering them around like some pint-sized dictator. Idly, Adam wondered how the small man stood upright with all that gold dangling around his neck.

Adam calmly walked across the street towards his target. As busy as the mini-pimp was, he did not sense Death's approach. The whores, however, noticed immediately.

"And what the hell you all looking at?" Juan snapped, still ignorant of Adam's approach. "Don't you back away when I'm talking to you! You all gonna listen to what I have to say!"

Adam tapped the little guy on the shoulder.

Juan spun. "And what the f-?" The pimp stopped suddenly and stared up in open-mouthed shock.

Adam smiled down. "Hello there, Juan. Can I have a moment?"

"Oh, hell no!" The little guy tried to run but Adam just grabbed him by the throat and slammed him to the ground. He then planted a foot onto Juan's chest and nodded towards the terror-stricken prostitutes. "Ladies," he said politely. "Would you excuse us? I need a word with Big Daddy, here."

They took the hint.

"You traitors bitches," Juan gasped.

"Don't you just hate it when people don't measure up?" Adam asked. He grabbed Juan by his oversized sports jersey and dragged the trash into a nearby alley.

"What did I tell you about those jokes?" Juan demanded, reaching into his belt.

Stripping the gun out of Juan's hand, Adam smacked the criminal's face with enough force to send him spinning into some nearby refuse. Looking down at the gun, Adam laughed. "A .22? Even your *gun* is tiny!" He threw the little weapon away.

Juan pulled himself out of the garbage and drew a knife. "God, I hate you!" he screamed and lunged.

Adam side-stepped the little guy's charge and grabbed his out-stretched arm, twisting the wrist. Juan yelped in pain and tried to kick but was blocked by the superior fighter. Adam then stepped in closer and, with a hand to the mini-pimp's chest, forced him to the ground.

"Are we done?" Adam casually asked.

Juan cursed at him in Spanish.

He punched the micro-man in the face. "How about now?"

"What the hell do you want *púto*?" the pimp demanded. "First you stop me from taking care of my business, now you start harassing me? What the hell did I ever do to you?"

"First of all, you weren't 'taking care of business' that first time, you were beating a fourteen-year-old girl who was whoring herself for you." Adam punched him in the face again. "Second, I'm not harassing you. When I *start* harassing you," the hunter then grabbed Juan's face in one weathered hand and pulled him in close, staring evil fire into the criminal's soul. "When that happens, you'll beg to get sent to prison and gang-raped by sixteen AIDS-infested Neo-Nazis just to get away from me." Adam tossed Juan back. "As for what you've ever done…?" he shrugged. "I just don't like you."

"It's a Mexican thing, ain't it?"

Adam blinked. "What? Shut up." He took the knife and stood. "Now do you want a little more of this ass-kicking, or you want to answer a few questions?"

Juan rubbed his nose sullenly.

"There was a break-in the other night. A couple was murdered in their home. Gruesome, slashed up. Nothing was stolen."

The criminal nodded. "Yeah, I heard. It was on the news."

"What I want to know is what you and yours have been saying. Who did it and why."

Juan shook his head. "Nothing," he said too quickly. "Nobody is saying nothing."

"Uh-huh." Adam crouched. "Ok. Here's how this is going to play out. You're lying to me. I really didn't think you'd know anything, I was just going on a hunch. But now I think you *do* know something."

"I don't!" the liar lied. "I swear I don't know nothing!"

"Yeah, that's possible. But I don't believe you. So, like I was saying, here's how we're going to do this. I'm going to ask you again and you're going to lie. Then I'm going to hurt you. You're scared of someone or something, so what I have to do is make you more scared of me. To do that, I'm going to have to mess you up." The hunter looked at Juan with dead eyes. "There will come a point when you can't take any more pain and you're going to tell me what you know. That's a fact. You have no control over *if* you're going to talk; you only have control over how much pain you endure *before* you talk."

Juan flinched away. "No!" he yelped. "Ok! Alright! Just, don't, alright? Jesus! What the hell is the matter with you? I know some cold people, but you got no soul!"

Adam stood. "Talk."

"That break-in," the criminal said, "that wasn't no break-in."

"Explain."

"Hear what I'm saying, *púto*. No truck outside. No people going in through windows or working the locks. A van pulled up to the driveway and some people got out. They were let in. No screaming. The way the news says it, that couple was did hard. But no screaming. And then the van just pulls away."

"How do you know about this?"

Juan said nothing, deliberately holding his lips together.

The hunter slowly drew his own large knife. "I'll count to one."

"Forget it."

"One." He moved in.

Juan emitted a high-pitched screech and flinched away. "Ok! Ok! Junior, alright! Junior told me!"

"Who or what is a Junior?"

Juan began trembling. "Junior, over at the Balls n' Styx. He runs everything now that his old man's at Telford."

"And why are you pissing yourself because of an inheritance?"

"Junior wasn't supposed to take over. He had a brother but..."

"His brother had an accident?"

"No, just... gone. Like the other people."

"What 'other people?'"

"Things getting weird out here. People taken off the streets. Nobodys right now. I've seen it happen. A white van pulls up, and you're gone. But that's changing. These people that night, they're somebodys. Something bad going on." The pimp made the sign of the cross, an act Adam found more than a little hypocritical.

He stood and walked away, leaving the small-time criminal lying in a growing puddle of his fear. Reaching the street, Adam turned towards the Balls n' Styx.

Before approaching the Balls n' Styx, Adam took a few minutes to circle the place, examining, noticing, and preparing. Although perhaps just his imagination, the building seemed to have more than a passing resemblance to a fortress. The entire lot was unlit and separated from the surrounding commercial properties by an unnecessarily-large parking lot. Security cameras monitored every avenue of approach. Large, industrial air-conditioning units roared in use like angry metallic guard dogs. A few expensive vehicles were pulled up to the back door, oriented outwards as though ready for a quick escape. Although graffiti decorated every surrounding building, the isolated, one-story structure itself was untouched. There were no windows, nor any other means of visible entry except for the small back door covered by iron bars and the large double front doors, both of which looked heavy enough to withstand a battering ram. This entertainment center looked to be the perfect place to set a trap.

Adam approached calmly and openly.

Once he was within ten paces, the front doors opened. From the darkness, the building blew a wave of machine-cooled air against the approaching intruder. Close behind, a lumbering wall of dark flesh emerged. He stood head and shoulders taller than Adam, with rolls of sweating flab hanging off a frame built for removing all unwanted things, from vehicles to people. Wisps of hair decorated a head that seemed to extend out of the shoulders without benefit of a neck. The stench coming off the guard was overpowering.

"You lost, mayonnaise?" the walking wall of blubber demanded in a voice that seemed to rise from his expensive-looking shoes.

With his left hand, Adam slowly reached into the side pocket of his white leather coat and retrieved a small packet of breath mints. Taking one for himself he offered the rest to the guard. "Please," he begged.

The behemoth smacked the mints from Adam's hand with a growl that ended in a gargle.

Clenched his throbbing hand, Adam said, "Alright, so we're not doing this the friendly way."

"You want friends, go online. Either way, fuck off."

"Look slim, I need to talk to Junior. He's inside. I'm going inside." Adam let his arms hang loosely on either side. "Move or be moved."

The mountain reared back with another gargle-growl and threw his punch. Easily anticipating the lumbering attack, Adam stepped into it, rolling his shoulder with the strike so that he was momentarily facing away from the target before driving his elbow into the mountain's middle and dropping his forearm into the giant slug's groin. He then leapt away and spun, facing his enemy, ready to continue the fight.

The guard, however, was not ready to continue. He dropped to his knees, looking disoriented. Wet, strangled sounds began rumbling up from within the monster, rising higher and higher.

"Ah, Hell," Adam noted and leapt aside.

Toxic sludge spewed out from the guard's mouth as he violently heaved. The monster's entire body spasmed with the force of the ejection. Adam watched with revulsion as seemingly gallons of what had once been food came flowing out of the beast's cavernous mouth. Finally emptied, the brute raised his head, gasping for breath, and looked at his attacker.

Adam reared back and smashed his fist into the guard's face, sending him into the pool of sludge. The hunter then turned away and entered the Balls n' Styx, taking only a moment at the entrance to grab a large bundle of napkins to wipe off his fist. He had to push a bit through the boundary between the natural air outdoors and unnatural chill within, leaning forward to penetrate the wall of cool air that battled against the Texas midsummer day.

Once inside, the hunter took a moment. The expansive and expensive sound-system dominating the far wall was silent. Opposite that waited a long bar, longer still than the Waystation's, guarding an even greater collection of alcohol. Rows of gaming tables stood arrayed like felt-covered warriors made of artificial wood in the center of the single room, and banks of pool cues lines the walls like weapons adorning a castle. Dark images of mechanical death and an afterlife free of anything Heavenly crawled along the walls and columns, whether in anticipation, celebration, or fear of what lay beyond life, Adam did not know.

A tall man wearing an expensive suit came walking into the main hall with an angry look as Adam stood within the dimly-lit room, framed by the blinding light coming from outside. "Delicious, what the f-?" He stopped, his dark eyes going wide at the sight of the racially-incorrect intruder standing at the entrance to his gaming den.

Adam glanced back through the open doors at the unmoving mound. "Really?" he asked blandly. "Delicious? Where the Hell do you guys come up with these names?"

"Who the hell are you?" the businessman demanded. His hand, weighted down with large, expensive rings, moved slowly towards his belt.

"Don't," Adam warned. He stepped towards the bar. "I'm only here to talk, Junior. I don't plan on spilling blood, but that can change if you go for your gun."

Junior paused a moment before letting his hand drop. "Who says I'm Junior?" His face took on an innocent look.

"Really?" Adam shook his head with a roll of his eyes.

Junior's wide smile fell just a little. "So, what can I do for you Mr.-?"

"Not to be lied to."

"Nice name." Junior joined his unwanted visitor at the bar, keeping a distance and his gun-hand free.

Adam spotted his preferred alcohol and reached across the polished bar, retrieving the bottle and a pair of glasses. He poured himself and his host a drink without asking, sliding the small glass across to Junior. "To honesty," he said, raising the drink.

Junior raised his glass with his left hand and drank. "I'm still waiting for a question."

"You're a criminal, Junior."

"And you're an asshole," the criminal replied with a shrug. "We've all got to be something."

"A little bird told me you had something to do with the MacAllister murders."

"This little bird have a name?"

"It might. Depends on what you have to tell me."

Junior grabbed a different bottle and poured himself and Adam another round. "I didn't have anything to do with that... business." He drank. "Nor did anybody who works for me."

"Any reason I should believe you?"

"Where's the profit? Cult killing? Ritual shit?" The criminal shook his head. "No money in that."

Adam considered. He had encountered any number of men like this before. A career criminal hwo would sell his own mother for the right price, and believed he held to a standard of ethics within the realm of the profitable. Seemed unlikely that Junior had anything to do with the killings; thus his honesty was, if not probable, at least possible. "Alright. What about the other kidnappings, the ones around Disante?"

"Same answer. Whoever is doing that shit has nothing to do with me. But I do know one thing."

"Which is?"

"They're using government vehicles, from the base. Not the big military ones that get painted up in camouflage, but those white ones that look like street rides."

Nondescript, government-issued vehicles. So cliché it might actually be true. If not, I can always come back and beat the truth out of Junior.

"About that little bird?" Junior prompted.

"You know a tiny pimp named Juan?"

"I used to," the crime lord replied coolly.

"Then we're done." Adam turned to leave, his second drink untouched. "As long as you've been honest with me, we have no other business." The hunter glanced back. "Otherwise, we'll talk."

Junior smiled wide. "You're always welcome."

5

$\mathcal{C}$andace was just opening the Waystation as Adam approached

the bar. The aging bartender had probably spotted him walking up the street before he could get within a dozen paces of the Waystation. She had that habit, Adam noted; as a creature of habit himself, he always arrived at approximately the same time and, for each of his arrivals, Candace would be at the window for some miscellaneous task. What made this instance unusual was that Adam had arrived well outside of his usual pattern, long before the sun had dropped behind the horizon; it was, in fact, barely at the apex of its daily journey. Despite the change, however, Candace still stood at the window, busying herself with a minor task and noting his approach with a raised eyebrow and a smirk.

She unlocked and opened the door for him. "Gettin' an early start?" she asked as Adam entered, leaning against the door for him to enter. This, also, was a change. Always before, the bartender had remained behind her bar. Always before, a solid piece of old wood had stood between Adam and Candace. Now, with the sun looking down, she stood very close. This change, one of so many recently introduced into Adam's unwanted life, made him start to sweat under his white leather coat.

He stopped at the door and glanced down at the new, more-provocative t-shirt she was wearing. It was solid white and the collar was an even deeper v-neck than before, with the bar's name curving across in deep red, the calligraphy enhancing the already generous apex of each breast. Tiny beads of perspiration, each a flawless gem catching the sun's rays, bound together across Candace's chest and slid down, guiding Adam's gaze down towards the mysteries within that form-fitting shirt. Given their proximity in that moment,

Candice's perfume was now a powerful pull rather than a subtle suggestion. "That's new," he noted, pausing in the doorway.

"Nope," she quipped, holding her position, looking up at him through heavy lids and breathing deeply. "Had them since puberty. Just got the shirt though." The outside heat was pushing at Adam, as though the day itself was encouraging something of which the man himself remained unsure. The midsummer breeze easily bested the feeble air conditioning, joining with the circulation of the Waystation's overhead fans to set the auburn ends of Candice's long hair drifting.

"Funny," Adam grumbled.

Candace shrugged and moved inside, sliding behind the bar while her hips did their usual dance in the tight, low-waisted jeans she always wore. With such a free viewing, Adam now had a better appreciation of that melodious rhythm. "Owner's idea," Candace was saying, snapping Adam out of the near-trance. The bartender pulled several bottles out of a box and stacked them behind the counter. "He figures that if I got them, I might as well use them."

Adam sat down at his usual stool, letting the familiar comfort of the natural oak and fake leather restore his sense. "Using that logic, you might as well go topless."

She glanced over her shoulder, arching an eyebrow at him. "You've got to leave somethin' to the imagination. A man likes to be teased, whether he admits it or not."

He just grunted, wiping beads of sweat from his brow.

Finishing her minor chore, Candace pulled a glass down from the overhead rack and placed it in front of Adam. "Usual?"

"Need something different from you," he replied. Adam softly placed a rough, callused hand over the glass, accidentally laying gentle fingertips on Candace's smooth skin.

The bartender paused, glancing down at their point of connection. Her deep breath paused, and it felt to Adam as though the Texas heat had been suborned by a greater one. He withdrew his hand.

Candace let her generous lips curl just a hint at the edge. She put a light hand over her heart, no doubt coincidentally tracing a few light fingers along the light coat of sweat that had beaded upon the bare skin of her chest. "Why Mr. Mysterious Stranger," she breathed, emphasizing her already heavy Texan accent. "You do set my heart aflutter. Dare I fear that you are about to suggest something tawdry and un-Christian?"

In truth, Adam was increasingly of two minds on that subject, the other mind speaking volumes at the moment. "Funny you put it that way," he muttered. "I need your help with some information, but you don't what to know what I'm going to do with it."

Candace took the glass, placing ice within and then filling it with water. "This about that girl from last night?" she asked, sliding the already-sweating glass in front of Adam.

He nodded, taking a long drink of the refreshing coolness. "You got me into something a lot deeper than some casual date-rape."

"What d'you need?"

"Trucks from Agarés were used, or are being used, to sneak on and off Fort Burleson. I need someone that can get me information on those trucks. Who got them, what they were used for, where are they now, who used them."

Candace thought for a minute, lifting Adam's glass to her lips, and using an agile tongue to fish out an ice cube. Adam said nothing while the bartender thoughtfully chewed, looking at him with unreadable eyes.

Amidst Adam's alcohol-assisted descent into self-loathing, the hunter had noted that Candace noticed and remembered things. She could pick out counterfeit twenties with barely a glance. Never once could Adam recall Candace consulting a reference to mix even the most obscure drink. She could tell when someone was lying.

"Might be one guy," she finally said. "Daniels, Jacob Daniels. Agarés Assistant Regional Dispatcher. Came in about a week ago, cryin' into his beer about some promotion he was passed over for."

Adam reached into the pocket of his white leather coat and pulled out a small wad of bills, placing it on the bar. "Thanks, Candace."

"You know," she said through the barest hint of a smile, a smile loaded with suggestion, "I was never sure if you knew my name."

Adam stopped before at the door, glancing back out of the corner of his sunken eyes. He could not look directly at the woman, but instead cast his sideways gaze only in her direction. At last, he said, "I knew it."

From the Waystation, Adam went to the Public Library. With help from a mousey librarian who kept glancing at Adam through unnecessarily-large glasses, he found a computer available for public use and logged up… or whatever. The librarian guided the technologically-deficient Adam through a few different web-places, providing a list of the more popular internet things on which people could proclaim their important opinions on unimportant matters. He could not help but shake his head in amazement.

Eventually, Adam found what he was looking for.

"Who's Jacob Daniels?" the librarian asked in a voice made almost silent from years of shushing people. She leaned in slightly to the glowing screen.

"Old high school friend," Adam casually lied, taking a small notebook and pen from the side pocket of his white leather coat and writing down the information.

"Trying to reconnect?" she asked adjusting again her large glasses.

Adam grunted an affirmative.

"Well," the librarian said, standing. "It looks like you've found what you need. Let me know if you have any problems." Adam thanked her as she turned to a waiting student.

Mr. Jacob Daniels, who was very excited about some books, television shows, and movies, was also kind enough to have put several pictures of his home on display. These included one with the house number, and another with a street sign.

Lord, what fools these mortal be.

Another internet search of various real estate sites the librarian had suggested, and something having to do with satellites taking pictures of the world, revealed that the address Adam had acquired was the correct one. He then went to the Agarés website and looked up several office phone numbers, writing them down on the small notepad. With all the necessary information, Adam logged down or whatever and left, giving a passing thanks to the mousy little librarian.

Agarés paid its employees well. As a mid- to low-level manager, Daniels should not have had that high a salary, and yet his house was spacious. Even in this newer, upscale neighborhood with its pristine playground, well-groomed lawns, and clean streets, the value of Jacob Daniels' house stood out. It was second-story, an oddity in central Texas, looked down on the neighbors. The backyard was fenced in with a tall, vinyl wall that further separated it from the surrounding chain-linked properties. Adam even spotted a pool, expansive deck, and hot tub during his slow circle of the area. Either Jacob Daniels was paid very well, or he was corrupt.

Standing at a nearby intersection, Adam pulled a disposable phone from the side pocket of his white leather coat and made the first call. "Finance," a female voice answered, "This is Alicia."

"Hey Alicia," the hunter lied in a pleasant voice, "this is John, over in Personnel. I was wondering if you could do me a huge favor. I've been trying to get hold of Jacob Daniels, over in Dispatch. I've had his file sitting in front of me for, God I don't even know, a week, I think. He was supposed to get some promotion, but for some reason he's not returning my calls. Could you check your files to see if you guys have gotten the updates on him yet?"

"Sure, hang on a sec..." The hunter heard typing in the background. "Couldn't you just check the financials from your computer?" Alicia asked.

"You know, I tried. For some reason, my whole damn system just keeps locking up every time I try to open anything but my own files."

"Ugh," Alicia sounded exasperated. "Tech Support really needs to get off their ass."

"Tell me about it. I haven't even gotten the last round of updates."

"What? That was two months ago!"

"I know!"

"I swear to God, you'd think they were sooo busy... oh, here it is." Another pause. "Sorry, it doesn't look like his 34s have gone through."

"Damn; I've up-putted that information three times! And the worst is he won't return any of my calls."

"Sounds like he doesn't want the extra money."

The hunter let out an audible sigh. "Hey, Alicia, could you do me a HUGE favor? I don't know what his deal is, but my supervisor is really riding me to get this off my desk. He's obviously not going to answer me, but maybe if someone else calls, and you've got that sexy phone-voice going. Do you think you could try calling him?"

"Sure," Alicia laughed. "I'll give it a try. Do you want me to just say that he needs to call Personnel?"

"Better yet," the hunter replied, "tell him he needs to change into his best interview clothes and get to the Personnel office for an interview fast. Let's make *him* sweat a little."

She laughed again. "I like it. If I can't get through to him, I'll try his supervisor."

"Thanks a bunch, Alicia."

"No problem." With that, she hung up.

Adam waited for about a quarter of an hour before making the next call. Finally, he dialed the second number.

"Dispatch," a squeaky, but technically male voice answered after multiple rings, "Lewis."

"Lewis, this is John, from Personnel, I need to speak to the manager."

"Just a minute." Some truly Hell-spawned music then forced its way out of the phone and into Adam's brain. Eventually another voice, this one nasal and dripping with self-importance, picked up.

"This is Mr. Kerns."

"Mr. Kerns, this is John, from Personnel. I've been trying to get in contact with Jacob Daniels for several days now with no success. Is he there?"

"No, he just left."

"Did he say when he'll be back? It's very important I get in contact with him."

"If you tell me what this is all about, I can get in contact with him."

"Thank you, sir. If you could just tell him that his promotion came through, but he needs to come to Personnel for a final interview? If he doesn't, then the promotion will pass to another candidate."

"I'll see to it he gets the message."

"Thank you, sir." The line went dead and Adam waited. Within thirty minutes, a car came howling up the street.

Hello Jacob Daniels.

The car shot through each stop sign, heedless of the law or the safety of any possible children in this family neighborhood. Adam waited until the car nearly skidded into Daniels' driveway before the hunter walked across the street. "Mr. Daniels!" he called out, pulling a pair of gloves from the side pocket of his white leather coat and putting them on.

"Not now!" the thin man yelled, not even glancing in the hunter's direction. Daniels looked very distracted. He did not even bother to lock his car, but instead walked with a burning intensity for his front door, fighting with his keys in a desperate attempt to figure out which one would grant him access.

The hunter continued walking up to the door. He watched as Daniels opened the door, still oblivious to his stalker's presence. The hunter stood at the front door until he heard the high-pitched beeping that indicated Daniels has disabled the house alarm and then acted. With his knuckle, the hunter began repeatedly pressing the doorbell so that it chimed incessantly through the house.

"Alright, alright, ALRIGHT!!!" Daniels began to open the front door.

The moment the hunter heard the door begin to open, he kicked it in with all his strength, sending the door flying into Daniels. The resulting impact forced the thin man to the floor of his tastefully decorated hallway with a thud. The hunter quickly darted inside, glancing back into the street to check for witnesses. Seeing none, he closed the door. Hearing Daniels groan, the hunter moved over, grabbed a fistful of black hair in one gloved hand, and delivered a solid punch to the man's already bruised face.

Jacob awoke to pain. A sudden slap in the face sped his return to consciousness but did little to steady his swirling mind. In a few moments, he realized he was sitting on a chair in his large, recently renovated kitchen with his arms painfully bound behind his back. He could not move his legs, either. He could barely breathe and began to panic, the wet air forcing itself in and out of his nostrils doing little to nourish his burning lungs. He tried to call out, but whatever was jammed into his mouth stifled the sound.

"Stop that," a harsh voice said from behind. Accompanying the word came a hard slap to the back of his head.

A man appeared from behind, moving around to face Jacob. He was built like a thug, with great strength in his arms and shoulders. He wore jeans and a plain black, long-sleeved t-shirt, odd for midsummer. Gloves covered his hands and a mask his face. Only his eyes were visible, eyes that stared out with no empathy or even humanity. The thug was looking down calmly at Jacob. "Ok," he said, "we're going to have a conversation now."

Jacob tried to speak but the gag prevented anything meaningful.

The thug held up a hand. "Yeah, I'll get to that," he said in a deep, gravelly voice that was as without feeling as were his eyes. He reached back, to the island counter, and picked up a picture of Jacob's smiling wife and two little daughters. "First, I want one thought in your mind. I want you to think of just one thing." He held the picture so close to Jacob's face, the man could make out the tiny gap in his youngest daughter's front teeth. "Do you want me here when they get home?" The thug then drove his fist into the picture.

Jacob started and violently shook his head.

"Good." He tossed the broken picture to the white-tiled floor and drew a large knife from behind his back. "Now, like I said, we're going to have a conversation. I have to take that gag out. Now, if you try to scream or call out for help, or any bullshit…" the thug held the blade a hair's breath away from one of Jacob's eyes. "If you try that, I will push this into your eyes, your ears, and cut out your tongue, but I won't kill you. I'll do all that and still have plenty of time to get away before any kind of help arrives. Do you understand?"

Jacob closed his eyes tightly and nodded, trying to control his bladder.

"Good." The monster straightened and pulled a long cotton tube from Jacob's mouth. The horrible creature then crossed the kitchen and, still holding the knife, pulled another chair forward so that he was sitting directly across from the terrified man.

"Alright, let's get one more thing very clear. I'm going to ask you questions. Some of them I'll already know the answers to. Those questions are to test you, to see if you're lying to me. If you try to lie to me, you start losing body parts. Understand?"

Jacob nodded.

"Say it."

"If I lie… I… lose body parts."

"Good." The thug leaned back in the chair, still holding his knife in plain sight. "What's your name?"

"Jacob Daniels."

"Where do you work?"

"Agarés."

"What job do you have at Agarés?"

"I'm the Assistant Regional Dispatcher. I control what vehicles go where."

"How many other Assistant Regional Dispatchers are there?"

Jacob hesitated, only a moment. "One," he finally replied. "One other."

"What happened to the other one?"

"What do you mean?"

The thug began to lean in, the knife coming towards Jacob's ear.

"He died," Jacob said quickly. "He… died, recently."

"When he died, did you have to do anything with his workload?"

Jacob said nothing, trying to think of options. The thug leaned forward and put the edge of the knife against Jacob's groin. "Don't even try it."

"I had to audit everything MacAllister had done for the past six months," he said very quickly.

"And you had orders, didn't you?"

Jacob nodded.

"Speak."

"I was told to approve MacAllister's last big order. No questions."

"The trucks?" When Jacob again just nodded, the thug motioned with the blade for more information.

"A government sedan, two vans, two SUVs, and an LMTV: a cargo-carrier. Already painted and stenciled. They were ready for shipping, but instead they were delivered to a private receiver."

"Who?"

"I don't know, it was redacted."

"Who ordered you?"

Jacob shook his head. His bladder had voided. "I can't; you saw what they did to MacAllister."

The thug leaned forward and pushed the point of the blade just slightly into Jacob's groin. "*They* are not here. *I* am here. Speak."

"Aubrey," he finally whispered, as though the name itself held power. "Lilith Aubrey."

6

*A*dam left Hector tied up in the kitchen without doing anything more permanent. The man had been too terrified of being exposed as an informant to call the police, so there was no need to clean up. The wife and daughter would take care of that.

As he moved on, Adam considered the new information. Lilith Aubrey. He recognized the name, of course. Although having only been in Disanté for a couple of months, Adam had heard of the woman. Anyone living within Meropis County knew who she was. As the Regional Vice President of Agarés, Lilith Aubrey held more power than any elected official, cop, or knife-toting former badass stupid enough to think he could help some random girl. Lilith Aubrey had the money, connections, and lack of anything resembling a soul enough to casually erase anyone she found irritating.

Since his arrival, Adam had heard more than a few whispered rants about Aubrey. Anyone who failed her was fired and blacklisted. A man who had bumped into her and made her spill a cup of coffee found himself unemployed, homeless, and under indictment for drug possession. Land her company needed for development was acquired, regardless of the daycare facility and low-income housing. There were even rumors of an unfortunate driver who had dented her car. *His* car had ended up pancaked between two Agarés semi-trucks. She had the power to destroy anyone that even casually annoyed her.

On the other hand, there's nothing better to do.

As Adam walked down the suburban sidewalk, he became aware of them. Two vehicles were following him. Two white SUVs with multiple passengers; one following behind, the other a few blocks ahead, waiting. He had been so lost in thought that he had walked into a trap. It was not yet complete, and Adam could escape; the surrounding yards all had the same low, chain link fences that offered innumerable routes. The more he thought about it, however, the more Adam realized that this situation offered him a chance for more information. Besides, now that he was aware of the trap, he had the advantage.

How best to use his advantage? Should he openly approach one of the vehicles and force a confrontation before the enemy was ready? Should he feign running to draw them into his own trap? Should he hold his position and force them to come on his terms? Each scenario had advantages and disadvantages, but nothing stood out in Adam's mind as the definitive offering of strategic excellence. Ultimately, he decided to do what would be most direct.

While continuing to walk down the empty street, Adam reached into the side pocket of his white leather coat and pulled out a packet of gum. On the rare occasion when he tried, Adam found looking helpless very difficult. Luckily, his new friends either chose to ignore this or were just stupidly arrogant. Moments before the white SUV behind him pulled up, Adam put a piece of gum in his mouth and grinned. Several hands reached out to grab him, pulling into the air-conditioned interior. He made some token resistance but allowed his abductors to win, the doors slamming shut and the vehicle moving on, past its idling partner. Truthfully, the ride and the A/C were not unwelcome.

Inside the vehicle, Adam had to fight his laughter. A man on each side held him securely between them. Each wore business suits and sunglasses, as did the two men riding up front. Through the reflection of the rearview, Adam could tell there were two more people behind him in a pair of those folding seats. An idle thought popped into his mind, wondering how comfortable those seats could be for grown men.

The one in the front passenger seat turned around and stared at Adam through his thick sunglasses. In response, Adam reached into the pocket of his white leather coat and pulled out his own sunglasses. Putting them on, he regarded his captors.

The passenger reached back and snatched Adam's sunglasses off. "Can we have a conversation?" he asked.

"Sure," Adam replied. "What about?"

"We want the girl."

"Tried online dating?"

"You need to take a moment to appreciate your situation. We have you. We can kill you at any time."

Adam glanced left and right, loudly chewing his gum. He just shrugged.

"We can be reasonable," Mr. Sunglasses continued. "We're prepared to compensate you for the effort you have expended in any way you feel is necessary. The only thing we ask is that you take the girl to some public place, any place you want, and leave her there."

"And I can have *anything* I want?"

Sunglasses nodded. "We have the power to grant you nearly anything.

Adam nodded. "I have to admit, that sounds pretty good." As he expected, the two holding his arms started loosening their grips. The corrupt were usually the quickest to believe others corruptible. Adam looked up and saw they are about to pass very close to a parked car. "On the other hand," he said, and spit his gum into the driver's ear.

The driver flinched away from the wet glob that impacted his ear and jerked the steering wheel. The vehicle turned in response, colliding with a parked car and spinning to a stop. Airbags deployed into a spinning chaos within the cab. Since the fools had failed to bind his hands, the hunter easily jerked free in the instant of the collision and braced himself. Having been the only person inside the cab that had not just been pummeled by an airbag or jerked back by a seatbelt, the hunter used the extra moments of clear thought denied his captors to draw his blade. He then proceeded to open the throats of the men on his left and right before they could even return to full consciousness. Hearing a rustle of movement from behind, the hunter bounced off the seat and spun in mid-air, pulling his knees up in the same motion. He faced the pair that had been sitting behind him and thrust out with both hands, one a fist and the other holding his knife. Already stunned from the crash, the two men could do little to stop their attacker from beating them further and slitting their throats.

A hand grabbed at his coat from behind. The hunter looked back and saw that Mr. Sunglasses had recovered. The hunter elbowed him in the chest. Turning, he grabbed the man's tie and jerked him forward, burying his knife in the eye. The driver groaned slightly, holding his head, but a quick slash of the knife ended that sound.

The hunter then forced the right door open and tumbled out into the fresh, hot air. The street was deserted, but he knew that could not last. The second SUV would have been following…

Shots rang out, impacting near Adam. Cursing his inattention, the hunter dove over the hood of the wrecked SUV. He laid down flat on the ground and looked under the vehicle. Three people had exited the second white SUV and were approaching him on foot, holding some variety of pistols at the ready.

At least they aren't assault rifles.

The backup team spread out, moving carefully as they approached the wrecked vehicles. Clearly, the primaries had underestimated their target, so now extra caution was required. Working in tandem, the three teammates moved in unison, each staying an equal distance from the primary transport and staying clear of one-another's line of fire. The diplomatic option seemed removed; this crash was clearly the target's response to the offer they had been instructed to deliver.

"What the hell?" the team member on the right called out.

"What have you got?" his partner on the left asked.

"He's gone!"

"What the hell do you mean he's gone!?! He *can't* be gone!"

The only female amongst them, blonde and cool, wearing a business suit and tie in defiance of the oppressive heat and danger, looked around. "Does anyone see him?" she demanded.

"He has to be here," the one on the left insisted, moving closer to the wreck.

"Hey," the female called out, "Stay where we can cover you."

No answer came from where their teammate used to stand.

"Jameson?"

Still nothing.

"*Jameson*!!!"

The remaining two looked at one another. Then a pair of sunglasses flew over the smoking transport, landing between them. The eye-protection had belonged to Jameson. Now they were cracked and covered in blood.

"Oh, shit!" the male gasped.

"At ease!" the female snapped, leveling her weapon at the wreck.

"No! Screw this!" the male backed away, moving towards the safety of their own, operational SUV.

"Get back here, you idiot!"

"Screw you, bitch!"

A knife flew out from the midday shadows, burying itself in the back of the male's neck. In response, the female ran around to where she thought, she hoped, to find the target, and fired at nothing.

"What the f-..."

A pair of hands grabbed her ankles and pulled, dragging the doomed woman off her feet. At the same time, the target pulled himself up, seemingly from the very pits of Hell itself, pinning her smaller frame down against the mass of his powerful body. His legs trapped hers, forcing them into an awkward pose that prevented anything but submission and his hands shot out, grabbing her wrists and forcefully holding her in place. Burning eyes bored into her face through disheveled hair and his filthy mouth twisted into a malicious snarl of clenched teeth.

She tried to struggle but, with the target pressing down on top of her, she could gain no purchase. She could barely even breath against the crush of his massive chest. He only stared hatred into her eyes and waited. They could both feel the frantic leap of her terrified heartbeat.

"Now's when you beg me not to kill you," he growled into her soul.

A fanatical tremor ran through her body. "Go to Hell. I die for *her*!" She worked at the pill hidden behind her cheek before biting down. In seconds, foam formed between her lips and dead eyes rolled back.

Adam cursed and jumped to his feet.

He had underestimated the resolve of the people he was facing. It had been a while since the hunter had seen such fanatical loyalty. Adam looked down at his own body before glancing up at the ever-advancing sun, now well into its descent. He took in the feeling of soreness and grime, not to mention the slight trickle of blood from a gash that had opened somewhere on his head. His overconfidence had cost him some minor injury, information, and most crucially of all, *time*.

7

"*You* what?" the receptionist asked for the third time. She was pretty, of course. Her hair and makeup were perfect, artfully arranged to enhance the girl's beauty while conforming to corporate sensibilities. She wore a tastefully revealing business skirt and blouse that was, while visually stimulating, not overly so; just the right amount of leg and cleavage on display for sexual objectification while enough remained concealed for a properly-conservative business setting. The receptionist stared up at Adam through her designer glasses, which she probably did not need, with a perfectly blank expression that would have stymied any other opponent. This girl was meant to frustrate the intentions of anyone who entered the building: a pretty, but immovable, gatekeeper.

"I said," Adam patiently repeated again, "I'm here to speak with Lilith Aubrey."

The receptionist, who never lost her perfect smile, looked Adam up and down. He could imagine the sight. Fresh from a car accident, admittedly of his own creation, Adam was filthy. He had cuts and bruises decorating his face and hands. Idly, he wondered if she was more critical of his faded jeans and t-shirt, his recent injuries, or just his general lack of hygiene. "Do you have an appointment?" the decorative roadblock asked.

Adam glanced around. Two guards were approaching from either side and behind. They wore Italian, designer-made henchmen suits. The clothes were so well tailored, in fact, that Adam almost could not notice the large firearms each had in their coats. The coloring of the henchmen matched the décor of the lobby.

Damn but they're pretty.

As the guards approached, Adam considered his options. The receptionist sat alone behind her large wooden desk with the Agarés logo carved in the front. He could not see her hands, which meant there was an alarm button, a gun, or both within easy reach of the smiling obstruction. Two more guards flanked her, standing far back in the corners of the massive, well-lit and air-conditioned reception area, with their hands folded in front of them. A pair of grand staircases curved their way around the walls of the room, up to the glass balcony above. Two more guards stared down at Adam from up there, making no effort to hide their hostility. Other than the large glass doors through which he entered, now blocked by a pair of well-dressed thugs, the only other way out of this cage seemed to be a pair of doors on the balcony above.

Grimly, Adam took a deep breath. The guards all had clear line of sight on him. The ones behind were being careful not to approach too close. The ones flanking the receptionist adjusted their position just enough to maintain clear lines from every direction. Professional. Disciplined. His current position was… unappealing.

Adam smiled and slowly pulled his hands free of his pockets, keeping them lose at his sides. "Lilith is expecting me," he evaded. "I represent Holly MacAllister."

The receptionist gave a rehearsed response, no doubt relieved to be back in familiar territory. "Ms. Aubrey does not meet with attorneys. If you leave your firm's contact information, along with whatever matter you are pursuing, our legal department will be more than happy to contact you at their earliest convenience."

Adam looked at her ID badge, strategically clipped at the bottom of her neckline. "Mindee?" he read, paying no heed to her artificially-enhanced cleavage. "Do I look like a lawyer?"

She again looked Adam up and down. "I'm sorry," she said, sticking to familiar conversational ground. "But unless you have legitimate, prearranged business with Agarés personnel, I'll have to ask you to leave." The guards were drawing within arm's reach.

"Mindee, I'm going to need you to dig deep here, ok? This is one of those situations that you're going to have to come out of the box on." Adam took a deep breath, slowing his heart rate and paying very close attention to his other senses while he looked and spoke to the obtuse receptionist. "I'm going to talk to Lilith Aubrey. Aubrey is going to *want* to talk to me. I'm not leaving… voluntarily, without that meeting. Now, if Aubrey finds out that something unfortunate happened here and she lost the chance to speak to me, especially when the name," he raised his voice slightly, "*Holly MacAllister* was involved… well that's going to be very bad for you.

"Now, I'm not asking you to do anything crazy like just let me walk in. All I'm asking is you call up to Aubrey's personal… whatever, aide, I guess. Ask him or her or it if Aubrey wants to have a little talk with me."

The receptionist never lost the smile on her pretty face, but she was clearly lost as to what to do. Fortunately, she was saved when a small phone, set aside from the two others on her desk, rang. "Excuse me," she said, turning to answer. In an amazing coincidence, the guards had all paused in their movements, some turning their heads slightly as instructions were delivered to the receptionist.

Adam glanced up at one of the security cameras. He waved.

The girl's conversation was brief. She turned back with her same, unwavering smile. "Ms. Aubrey would like to speak with you, sir."

"Fancy that."

She gestured at one of the two guards flanking Adam. "If you'll just follow them?"

One of the guards moved around the desk, leading Adam, the other stayed behind him. The receptionist pressed a concealed button beneath her desk and the wall behind her parted, revealing a moving walkway.

"Nice," Adam noted to the unresponsive guards. "Very 'secret lair.'" He obediently followed his escort forward.

As so often happened amidst the vast expanse of Central Texas, rather than building *up*, Agarés had built *out*, necessitating an extended trip from the main entrance to nearly any destination. As their corporation expanded, so too did their original headquarters. A sprawling complex of interconnected, crisscrossing hallways, rooms, and dark passages covered more than ten acres of what had once been a picturesque prairie. Beginning as a shipping business before industrialization, the Agarés Corporation had grown, spreading out into multiple venues from energy production and agribusiness, to weapons and chemical research. Although their corporate headquarters had long since moved on to New York like any good multibillion-dollar military-industrial complex, Texas was their traditional seat of power, and the Meropis Building, though not on the coastline, still had a strong echo of the company's shipping past.

Agarés began in this area, dealing in illicit goods, arms, and slaves during the bloody conflicts between the various colonizers wanting to claim sovereignty over what would one day become Texas, and it remained a hub for their activities. Research, personnel training, important conferences, long-term storage, and product demonstrations all took place under the careful gaze of the Meropis Building. Only the most elite of the business world were even allowed through the front doors. They, and now Adam.

The long walkway eventually led to the center of the Meropis Building. Most of the trip was spent in an enclosed, only dimly-illuminated tunnel, as though they moved through some abyssal tunnel. Occasional revealed side passages opened into other areas, each marked with small, overhead signs. Adam half expected one to read: Abandon Hope, Ye Who Enter Here. After several minutes of travel, they at last reached the doors of a private elevator. Without a button being pushed, the doors parted revealing a cart with walls made entirely of mirrors.

Adam looked down and, noting the reflective floor as well, snorted. "I bet that's real popular with women wearing skirts."

The heavy doors slowly closed, and the cart began to rise. There were neither controls nor indicators to reveal their progress. Even the music that should have gone with their trip was absent. Adam leaned forward slightly, looking at himself in the mirrored doors and realized how long it had been since he had shaved.

The doors parted, and they exited into a wide hallway made of dark wood. The carpet looked expensive, and there was an unnecessary fireplace to combat the chill of the heavy air-conditioning. A set of double doors, of wood inlaid with gold, sat opposite the elevator. Along the walls on both sides were long sets of windows looking down on the city of Disanté. From the height, Adam guessed that they were on the tenth floor. Surprising, since the Meropis Building had thirteen.

In the center of the hallway was a large desk with another pretty receptionist. This one was different than the window dressing up front. She was older, for one; while a lot of money had been spent to hide the fact, the weight of years could be seen in how this one carried herself. Wrinkles could be hidden with cosmetics and a body could be kept trim and appealing with surgery and exercise, but the thousands of small movements someone makes betrays such conceits. Her blonde hair was styled, the dye probably supposed to preserve some youthful radiance. More than that, however, were the eyes; this woman's eyes spoke of years beginning to stack upon each other, and her desperate battle to hold them off.

"Good afternoon," she said in a firm voice, moving around the large desk set to one side of the hallway with an exaggerated and well-practiced sway of the hips. Everything about this woman screamed of her desperate need to hold a man's attention. "My name is Isabel Hollman, I am Ms. Aubrey's assistant." The assistant held out her manicured hand.

Adam just stood there with an empty expression, not bothering to take her hand.

Hollman did not lose the neutral smile but let her hand drop. Instead, she used the hand to gently smooth the front of her grey blouse, running her fingers slightly down the front. Adam ignored her unspoken invitation to look down, but kept his gaze locked on her cold brown eyes.

Disappointed, the assistant let her hand drop. "Well," she said, "I'm sure you're anxious to begin your meeting. May I take your coat?"

"No."

"Can I get you something? Scotch? Plain Water?"

"Also no."

"Well in that case." Hollman took a few steps but paused and gestured towards one of the guards. "If you'll just hold out your arms…?"

"Still no."

"It's a standard security precaution," she lied. "We just have to make sure you're not carrying anything dangerous."

"Like the weapons he's carrying?" Adam asked, nodding towards the guard that had approached him. He looked back at his other escort. "Or the ones *he's* carrying?" And at Hollman. "Or the one *you've* got?" His look went to the side of the sheer business suit she wore, noting where the coat caught despite the careful tailoring to try and hide a gun holster.

"How about we cut through the bullshit?" Adam suggested. "I've got weapons, you've got weapons, and I'm betting when I get in there, Aubrey will have weapons. I'm here to talk about some illegal things your boss has been doing and some illegal things I've been doing. So, stop wasting everybody's time, open the damned doors, and let's get going."

There was a light click and the doors opened.

Adam brushed past the startled assistant and entered Aubrey's office. As he expected, it was massive. Large windows dominated three of the walls, giving the business executive a good view of her domain. The woman herself sat behind her large wooden desk, which was raised up a few inches higher than the rest of the floor. A set of three chairs rested in front of the dais and Adam walked over and sat down in one of these without invitation.

Lilith Aubrey was an average looking woman, if one looked only with the eyes, rather than the mind. She had light brown hair tied up in a bun that did nothing to enhance her plain looks. What little time she had spent on makeup seemed to make her look more like a schoolteacher than a business executive. Her suit was obviously expensive but did not flatter her narrow frame, and the few pieces of jewelry seemed out of place, despite their obvious cost. Her narrow, dark-framed glasses rested low on her pointed nose, and her boney hands were steepled over her mouth.

"I know you, Adam Kadmon," she said in a low voice.

Adam froze. The entire scenario he had prepared for this encounter vanished in an instant. He began reevaluating the potential threat of this person.

"I know what you are now," she continued. "I have some idea of what you once were, and who you once worked for. I've been having you watched ever since your encounter with Sergeant Isandro and Mister Simon upon your arrival in Disante."

Adam did not respond. The hunter heard Hollman and the guards enter and close the doors behind them. He was aware of the two men moving to opposite sides of the room and the receptionist standing against the door. He breathed very slowly and waited.

"I've been very curious if the reports were true, that you were just going to drink yourself to death. I wondered if there could be anything that would make you take an interest in my territory. Something has."

Adam noticed a pad of paper on Aubrey's desk and took it. He took a pen as well and wrote something down. Once finished, he wordlessly tossed the pad over to her and sat back down, looking intently at the woman.

Aubrey picked up the pad and looked at what he had written, the hard lines and pin-point stars that made up the script of the First Language.

She lifted her eyes back to Adam and smiled. "I'm sorry," she said, "I can't read this… yet."

Adam leaned back in the chair and smiled back. "Then you don't know anywhere near as much as you think you do." He glanced back at the painting above Aubrey's bar, an image of Dark Angels flying over the Earth, spreading evil to humanity. He shook his head and chuckled to himself. "So, which one have you been talking to? Haziel? Glasyalabolas? Balberith? I don't really care, I'm just curious."

Adam kicked both filthy boots up onto Aubrey's absurdly expensive, and immaculate, desk. With all that he had seen, he felt that he now had a good understanding of the type of people he was dealing with. Unfortunately, the hunter had met this kind many times before. "Let me guess," Adam mused aloud, "wealth, power, in your case knowledge, maybe beauty. It's been promising all sorts of things to you in exchange for… what? Blood sacrifice? Sex rituals?"

Aubrey said nothing. She did not even move.

"And it probably began innocently enough. You stumbled on it, or were introduced, and it gave you a few tidbits of information. Very useful things that made you powerful, wealthy, but not quite satisfied. It didn't ask for anything at first, just to keep having conversations. Eventually, it asked for a little something in return, probably just animals at first, maybe a little ritual involving a little taboo-breaking. When it started offering more in exchange for just a few small sacrifices… well, you figured since you've already come so far, and it had already kept so many promises, why not?"

Aubrey leaned forward. "You of all people should understand the power that can come from one of them," she said. "And they ask so little in return."

"Oh sure. All you had to do was brutally murder a husband and wife."

"I murdered no one."

Adam looked flatly at her. "Are you *really* going for a semantic argument?"

Aubrey stood and moved around her large desk, towards the bar. "Mr. Kadmon," she said as she walked, "in order to succeed here at Agarés, one must have a certain moral flexibility."

"You mean it's a pit of snakes and the only way to survive is by being the most venomous."

"Indeed. I have accomplished much through basic treachery, but I have reached the limits. You have no idea how many people involved in business these days have sold their souls."

"You'd be surprised what I know."

She selected a bottle of no doubt expensive booze along with two heavy glasses. Carrying these, she returned to her desk. "That raises an interesting point. Anyone with true power understands one simple fact. The greatest type of power is information." She set one empty glass in front of Adam and poured him a drink before pouring one for herself. "You, sir, despite having severed ties with your… former employers, are a nearly limitless source of valuable information." She leaned against her desk, sipping her drink and eyeing Adam closely.

"No."

Aubrey held up her hand. "Please hear me out. Your only interest in my affairs stems from the girl. That is correct, is it not?"

Adam just raised an eyebrow.

"My only interest in the girl is due to certain… obligations I must fulfill. While failing to live up to those obligations would have certain repercussions for me, *you* would know how to avoid those. I would get to keep what I have gained, without having to pay any sort of price. I, therefore, propose a trade. If you help me break my deal and escape any consequences of doing so, I will cease hunting the girl and release the life insurance funds of her parents. With that money, she will be able to start a new life anywhere she desires." She returned to her chair and sat, holding an unblinking stare at Adam.

He stood, returning the unwavering stare. "I'll think about it," he said after several heartbeats. "In the meantime, call off your dogs."

"You have until eleven o'clock tomorrow night to give me a positive answer," she replied. "Otherwise, I will send my people for the girl. I guarantee that not even you, with all your skill, will be able to stop them all."

8

"What the hell?" Adam had arrived home to madness. The dust that insulated his few pieces of furniture was gone. The cheap, plastic linoleum of his floor shined. Pictures had been hung on the walls and the walls themselves had been cleared of their various stains. Adam could no longer see out his window due to the curtains that now, for some bizarrely feminine reason, covered the exterior view. Several new... devices of some arcane kind rested in his kitchen. Adam had no idea what their purpose was, but their presence chilled his unwanted soul. Worst of all, some horrific stench hung in the air, clogging Adam's lungs with the sweet, cloying scent of flowers. As he stood in this bewildering swirl of feminine order, a chilling thought entered Adam's mind.

So, *this* is my Hell.

Adam stood in his doorway for some unmeasured time, frozen in shock, fearing that his inevitable fate had finally happened. He was numb to the shifting wind around him as the cool air from a large fan and merrily-blowing air conditioner raged against the swirling heat from outside, both forces struggling around Adam as he, himself, fought to understand what his senses registered around him.

Finally realizing that he had not yet descended into the Pit, Adam retrieved enough sense to become properly vengeful. "What?" he sputtered. "Where?" Words failed the battle-hardened warrior at the sight of this madness. He blinked in confusion and checked the address on the doorframe in the desperate hope that he had somehow stumbled into the wrong apartment. His hope was in vain, however; he was... home. "Who?" he finally sneered, narrowing his eyes and searching for the target of his newest-born rage.

Holly came dancing out of the bedroom, oblivious to the presence of her seething, snarling, surely benefactor. The girl was barefoot, kicking her short legs in cheerful, feminine glee at having violated the masculine sanctity of Adam's lair. All she wore was one of his dress shirts, which for her may as well have been a full dress. The sleeves were rolled up to her tiny elbows and a handkerchief bound the girl's dark mass of hair back into a loose ponytail. The peppy little queen bee had cleaned off all her ruined makeup, and the chocking stink of wet hair, powerful enough to override even the stench of aromatherapudic poison clogging the air, suggested little miss workaday had bathed. Little white things were stuck in Holly's ears. Adam assumed whatever was wired into her head was playing music since the perky little princess was rhythmically gyrating her undeveloped ass and mumbling something about not needing a man.

"Hey!" Adam barked.

Holly shrieked and jumped into the air, twisting into some strange, convulsive shape before returning to the ground. When the girl saw who it was that stood in the doorway, she let out several deep breaths of relief. "You ass!" she exclaimed with a hand to her small chest. "You scared me to death!" The girl tore the white buds out of her ears, putting them into her pocket with an obvious intent to chastise Adam for his lack of courtesy. She stopped however, upon getting a good look at her storm-faced guardian. "What happened?" she gasped.

"Funny," he growled in response. "I was about to ask you the same question."

Holly ran forward and put a hand out but stopped, clearly hesitating for fear of causing more pain. "Oh, my God," she whispered. "What *happened?*"

"I fell," he replied, twisting his neck until it made a loud crack. Adam dropped the large bag he suddenly remembered he was holding and walked to the kitchen counter.

Holly, ignoring the bag, closed the front door. "Is this... because of me?" Her voice became very small.

"No," Adam replied sarcastically. "I just happened to get jumped by a random biker gang, dragged through a construction site, and pissed on an electric fence, all on the same day that *you* entered my life." He looked around the counter helplessly. "Where the hell is my cup?"

She pointed to the overhead cabinets. "I put the cups up there."

Adam growled and turned and yanked the cabinet open but paused at the array of glassware. "Explain," he said darkly.

She cautiously walked up behind him. "What? You only had one cup and it had mildew in it."

Adam said nothing, but only made more sounds of discontent and reached up for one of the offensive glasses. Pain stopped him, however. He barked in protest as a knife of agony stabbed into his side, bringing a hard reminder of the day's activities. Adam quickly turned and leaned back against the counter, breathing deeply as he forced the pain back down into a corner of his mind where it could be ignored.

"Is it bad?" Holly asked, her tiny voice thick with worry.

His eyes snapped open in anger, a thousand hateful retorts ready to blister the foolish girl's soul. Each one of them, though, died on the tip of his tongue. Adam looked at his young charge and saw the fear and uncertainty she obviously felt, made all the worse for the pain her guardian had obviously suffered on her behalf. He stood straight, emptying his face of any discomfort. "I've had worse."

"Can I help?"

"I'm fine," he lied. To prove it, Adam again tried to reach for a glass but was again stopped, biting back a painful curse.

Holly recognized his discomfort and put a soft hand on his arm. "Please let me help."

He turned with renewed anger, ready to establish the obedience of his unwanted guest but again was halted. Holly looked up at him with large eyes, wide and shining in concern. Adam sighed deeply. "Fine."

He awkwardly moved to the couch. There, he carefully sat down, grumpily moving the pointless pillows. "Water," he commanded.

Holly nodded but put away the glass she had already retrieved. Instead, the girl reached into Adam's refrigerator and brought her guardian a plastic bottle. When he took it and glanced up at her in curiosity, she smiled. "You'll like this," she insisted.

"What's wrong with the tap?"

"Ew," she replied, making a face.

Adam shook his head but drank deeply from the bottle. He grumbled an acknowledgment of the clean flavor. He then slowly, carefully, removed his white leather coat.

"Oh my God!" Holly gasped. She could not help the exclamation.

Adam glanced up, noting his reflection in the absurdly-large television that now dominated his wall. The reflection was unfamiliar, not only for how rarely he bothered looking at his strange face, but also for the evidence of his day's activities. Before him, the man's front was a gory mess. While his face showed many cuts and bruises, mute evidence of the violence of the day, his body was much worse. His t-shirt was torn in several places, and deep bruises were clearly visible. Some blood had trailed from injuries on the man's head and neck, but more had sprayed on him from some unknown target. An ugly bruise, deep purple with flecks of yellow, peaked above his neckline. "What," Adam calmly asked the shocked Holly, "you've never seen real violence before?"

She just shook her head slightly. "Shouldn't you go to a doctor or something?"

"Or something." He took another drink of water and leaned his head back. "By the way," Adam grumbled, gabbing a thumb towards the pack that still rested near the door. "I got your stuff."

Holly said nothing, only looked at the deep gash on the back of his hand. "Has that even been sterilized?"

"You're just not getting off this, are you?"

"Wait here," she commanded and went into Adam's bathroom.

"Uh, it's *my* apartment," he said to the empty room. "I'll leave if I want." He chose to remain seated.

Within moments, Holly returned with a small box and some small towels, sitting down on the now-clean coffee table. Without a glance to Adam, she began rummaging through the contents of the first aid kit.

She removed a plastic bottle and held it against one of the small towels, briefly upending it, then turned to her patient. "Take off your shirt."

"What? No."

"Stop being such an ass. It looks like you got shit-kicked by a pack of coyotes! You can't even raise your arm without whimpering like a little girl!"

"I can to!"

She sat back and crossed her arms.

"I don't feel like it."

"Uh-huh. Shut up, stop being stubborn, and take your stupid shirt off so I can make sure you're not going to die."

"Look," he grunted," I'll be fine in a few hours. Just leave it alone, will you?"

The tiny, tyrannical girl just sat there looking down at her protector with queenly resolve.

He grudgingly complied, grumbling that he did so only because it suited him.

"Oh," Holly started, again given pause at the sight of Adam's extensive tattooing. Now, however, his body was decorated with evidence of violence to match the evidence of his past. The bruises only hinted at before were revealed to trail all the way down his broad chest, matching almost perfectly the dark color of the ritual markings. More bruises, worse than the first, crossed the muscles of his stomach, winding their way behind to his thick back.

"Are you going to stare," he asked, "or do something about it?"

The girl shook aside her shock and nodded. She gently took his hand and lowered the moistened towel towards it. "This might sting a little," she warned.

Adam did not reply, nor did he make any sound or reaction at all as she cleaned the wound. "You fell, huh?" Holly asked lightly, continuing to work.

He only grunted, snorting a bit at an inside joke.

"What happened to the other guy?"

"Fell harder."

Reapplying the antiseptic to the towel, Holly cleaned the small cut on the back of Adam's neck, which the hunter had not even noticed. Throughout, he gave no sign of discomfort, keeping his even breathing and expression steady. Once the cuts were as clean as she could get them, Holly retrieved several bandages and placed them over the wounds. Seeing this done, she looked at the series of bruises and sighed. "Turn around."

Adam obeyed.

The girl retrieved an ointment from the first aid kit. Adam could tell there was something, some question, on her mind. As she worked, Holly kept making as though to speak but stopped before forming the words. He could tell she needed to know something but feared the knowing. Several silent, increasingly awkward minutes went by before she finally whispered, "Why?"

"Just clean," he answered.

"You don't even know me," she could not help but continue as her hands worked the salve into the muscles of his back.

He said nothing as she cleaned and then rubbed ointment along the length of his injuries. They were both quiet for a time as she worked to soothe his hurt. Holly eventually began lightly massaging the ointment onto the bruises that marred his lower back.

"If you want...," she finally said as her hands worked on one of the large injuries above his hip, "I mean, if you're looking for something in return..."

"No," Adam snapped, turning his head slightly towards her. "There's enough people trying to use you," he almost growled.

Holly sat back and let her hands fall to her lap. "Then why?"

Adam stood. "It needs to be done."

"What does that even mean?"

"It means my reasons are my own," he replied in a voice thick with warning. "You're getting what you want, so don't question."

"You make it sound like I'm using you."

Adam titled his head slightly and opened his weathered eyes wide. "I don't know what I'm going to do," he said mockingly, holding his hands up as though helpless.

Holly narrowed her eyes. "Are you accusing me of manipulating you?"

"Do you have a vagina?" he asked flatly.

"Oh my God!" the girl leapt to her feet in defense of her gender. "You are such an ass! Women are not all manipulators!"

"Yeah," Adam replied, turning back towards the kitchen, "I'll be sure to tell Eve that the next time I see her."

"You know what?" Holly shouted with tears beginning to shine in her eyes. "Screw you! I didn't ask you to help me!"

He spun and pointed a finger at her. "And I didn't ask you to destroy my apartment!"

"Destroy!?! I *cleaned* it, you... you..."

"I'm waiting," he replied calmly.

Holly steadied her expression and stance. "You lonely, pathetic, misogynistic, misanthropic, *ass*," she finished.

Adam got red-faced and took an unconscious step forward. With great care, the muscles in his face twitching with the desperate effort he exerted to control his rage, he replied "I am not... pathetic."

The girl just sniffed and moved over to her bag, opening it, and rummaging through the contents.

"Hey!" he barked. "Do you want to focus here?"

"I'm sorry, were you still talking?" She was clearly paying little heed to her guardian's tantrum.

"I want an explanation."

"To what," she all but yawned, still taking an inventory of her meager possessions.

"To what!?!" he demanded. Adam angrily gestured around his now-spotless home making inarticulate sounds of rage.

"What?" Holly asked. "This place was gross and I was stuck here, so I cleaned up."

"With what?" Adam almost screamed. "I don't even have a broom!"

"Uh, yeah," she replied with a roll of the eyes. "I noticed. But you do have neighbors."

"You went to the neighbors!?! What kind of idiot are you?"

"Oh, calm down. I didn't leave the building and I didn't talk to *every*body. There was just one kid. One of your neighbors has a son who has a car."

"YOU LEFT!?!"

Holly looked up at Adam in irritation. "You know, I'm right here. There's no need to yell."

"I've been out there," he growled through clenched teeth, "I've been threatened, insulted, shot at. I got into a wrestling match with a walking mountain. I've been in a car wreck and an alley fight. And while I've been trying to keep you alive, you went out to buy window cleaner!?!"

"Don't be stupid. I gave the kid a list and some money."

Adam rubbed his temple, his voice going flat. "Why would some random kid go supply shopping for you?"

"Simple," Holly grinned. "He was stupid and horny and all I was wearing at the time was a towel." She held up two fingers close together in front of her eye. "A *really* small towel."

"You showed your ass to get a kid to go shopping for you?"

"No, I just let him think that I *might* show it when he came back."

Shaking his head, Adam walked towards his bedroom but stopped at the door. "Why the hell are all those pillows on my bed?" he demanded.

Holly came up behind him and smiled. "Don't you like it?"

Adam realized that he had picked up a slight twitch in his left cheek. "Do I look like a person who's happy in his surroundings?" he asked in a deathly calm voice.

"I was just trying to be doing something nice," the girl said in a tiny voice, her large eyes going wide in a look of pure innocence.

Horrible, agonizing pressure threatened to squeeze Adam's brain to mush. He waged a battle with his temper, forcing down any one of a hundred vile comments demanding to be roared at this tiny engine of chaos who had stampeded into his life. His whole body shook with the need to throw something, probably the girl, through something else. Battle was something the hunter knew how to deal with. Destruction and carnage he could handle with skill and grace. Violence was the only area the hunter felt any comfort with and now, somehow, Adam found himself in as alien a situation as possible.

Adam half-turned, ready to renew the argument. He took a step forward with fists clenched. His face was bright red and veins stood out on his temples and neck. Holly's reaction was like a bucket of icy water thrown in his face. She had taken a step back. Her already pale face had lost even more color and her wide eyes grew wider. A slight tremble shook her tiny frame even though the girl tried to stand firm in the face of her enraged protector.

More than anything else though, was the look in Holly's eyes. Fear shone in those dark pools. Looking at Adam, she was terrified. Even more than the fear, more than seeing his own irrational image reflected, he saw the awful look of betrayal... again.

Adam had thought to lose those wounded eyes in drink, to at last be free of his great failure. Those large, dark eyes that had looked at him with hope, that had plead for help. Adam had looked into those eyes even as the light faded, as his awful failure came crushing down on his unwanted soul. And now, years and miles later, he saw the same look of betrayal, the same overwhelming fear and accusation in a new set of eyes, new and yet, somehow, the same. Here, again, an innocent needed his help and, again, he was failing her.

Shit. If she starts crying, I'm going to kill myself and save Hell the wait.

"I'm glad my feet don't stick to the floor anymore," Adam muttered. His entire body visibly, forcibly relaxed, shoulders slumping, fists unclenching, and his face twisting into something less than a frown. He looked down and away, unable to meet Holly's gaze.

The girl sniffed loudly. "It did take a lot of work," she said with wide eyes that just barely held back a flood of almost entirely sincere despair. She continued to look at her reluctant protector expectantly.

Adam made a sound that was part sigh and part growl. "And the pictures of the paintings aren't… awful… I guess." He turned back and held a finger up. "But I don't need all those damned pillows."

"Oh, they're not for sleeping," she assured him, "they're just for decoration."

Adam was about to ask a very stupid question about the purpose of decorative pillows but, realizing the futility, opted to change the subject. "Get dressed. We've got some things to talk about and I need a drink."

Holly nodded and went back to her bag.

Adam moved to his bathroom but was again stopped by the sight that welcomed him. Something was giving him another headache. He did not know if it was the dizzying array of colors, the decorative crescent moon soaps, or the mixtures of flowery goodness mixed with ammonia cleanser that forced itself into his nostrils. Something in his bathroom caused him great pain. Then he spotted the source: something fuzzy was covering his toilet seat... which was down.

Adam hung his head and choked back a sob.

9

They arrived at the Waystation as the sun was dipping below the horizon. The bar was empty except for Candice, who spotted their approach from the window and greeted the pair with her usual half-smile. Rather than occupying his usual stool, Adam sat down at a booth in the back corner. He knew that once the sun finished its descent and the temperature began to drop, the various patrons would begin to filter in, and he had no desire to be overheard.

Holly wordlessly sat down opposite her gruff benefactor, smoothing the back of the grey skirt she had eventually chosen to wear. Despite Adam's assurances that nobody cared how she looked, the girl had still spent an insane amount of time preparing for their trip. Apparently, it was impossible for any female to leave her den without going through an elaborate ceremony of choosing clothes, brushing hair, applying makeup, and doing other woman-things before finally announcing that all was ready for the short walk to the bar.

Candice came over to their booth with a bowl of peanuts. She had not bothered with the ball cap yet in the late-afternoon heat; instead letting her long hair flow free in the idle breeze generated by the overhead fans. The bartender had a carefully neutral expression as she looked down at the odd pair, but satisfaction clearly shown through her eyes to see Adam still looking out for Holly. "Your usual?" she asked the gruff man.

Adam hesitated a moment but then replied, "Not tonight, I'm the designated ass-kicker."

"What about you, honey?"

"A highball."

"No."

Both women looked at Adam. He looked flatly at Holly. "You're nineteen and you're not drinking."

Holly sunk down in her seat, sticking her lower lip out a bit. "You know how to make a Cinderella?" she asked sullenly.

"Comin' right up," Candice replied with a smile, returning to the bar.

Holly leaned in, looking at Adam with a curious expression. "How the hell do you know how old I am?"

"While you were passed out last night, I cut you in half and counted the rings." He picked up a small handful of peanuts. "Also, it was on your real ID." He crushed the peanuts with a casual flexing of his fist.

"You went through my stuff?"

"I saved you from a rapist," he replied, casually sifting out the seeds, "and brought you to my place where you promptly threw up and passed out on my couch. Call me curious to find out your name, at least." Adam casually brushed the discarded shell pieces onto the floor and reached for fresh ones.

"Yeah well… at least I cleaned up."

"And then some."

Candice arrived with their drinks, giving Adam a glass of sparkling water and ice. She wordlessly put them down and left, giving the pair the privacy they obviously sought.

Adam stared at the concoction in front of Holly. It was in a highball glass, tall and narrow, but it looked and smelled like some kind of fruity nightmare. "What is that?" he asked.

Holly took a sip and smiled. "It's a Cinderella," she replied. "Orange, pineapple, lemon, soda and just a little sugar." She took another sip and made a yummy sound. "Damn, this is *really* good." The girl raised her glass towards Candice in gratitude and smiled. The bartender nodded back.

"Christ," Adam noted, afraid he might get diabetes just from the smell. "Anyway, like I said before, we have some decisions to make, and by *we*, I mean *you*."

Holly nodded.

Adam briefly laid out the situation. He told the girl about Lilith Aubrey's offer to him for employment and amnesty for Holly. "We've got until eleven tomorrow night to give her an answer," he continued. "If we say yes, then you go free. If we say no or just don't answer in time, Aubrey sends her goons after you in force."

"But she doesn't know where I am."

Adam shook his head. "We can't assume that. She said she knew who I was. She was probably bluffing about knowing who exactly I was, but she might know enough. We have to assume she's having me watched, which means she would know where you are."

"How do you know you're being watched?"

He rubbed the back of his very sore neck. "I've had hints today the bad guys know how to find me."

"Don't mess with it," Holly cautioned absently before taking another sip of her sugar.

"Where did you learn about treating wounds?"

"You mean first aid?" she corrected. "I was a lifeguard for two summers."

Adam grunted. "We can try getting you out of town," he said, returning to the subject. "Unfortunately, with the resources Aubrey has, there's just no safe bet you can get away."

"So, what are my choices?"

"Run, hide, deal, or fight." Adam pulled from his drink and continued foraging for peanuts. "Run and she'll find you. It's only a matter of time. Same for hide; Aubrey has too much control in this town."

"So that leaves deal or fight?"

Adam nodded. "If it comes to a fight, we'll lose. She has too many people that are either too loyal or too afraid of her to back down. Sooner or later… we'll lose."

Holly took another sip of her fruity drink. "It sounds like my only choice is to deal."

"Sometimes life is like that."

"But what about my parents?" she demanded. "I deal, I walk away with money and whatever, but that bitch Aubrey gets away with killing my mom and dad?"

Adam shook his head slightly. "Like I said, sometimes life is like that. Aubrey owns the authorities in this town. She's above the law. And she's too well protected for any chance at vengeance." Almost without thinking, he slowly extended his hand and took hers. "I won't tell you what to do. Whatever you decide, I'll back you. But it has to be your decision."

"It's not right," Holly whispered, tears standing in her eyes.

"It's not."

The girl sniffed loudly and looked around. "I've got to clean up," she announced. "Where's the little girl's room?"

"I don't know," he admitted, but jabbed a thumb back towards the rear. "Shitter's down that way."

Holly rolled her eyes and stood, walking back towards the small hallway and mumbling, "Ass."

Candice walked over, handing Adam a fresh drink. "So, this'll be over soon?"

"Not the way she would've hoped," he replied with a nod, "but better than it could have."

The bartender put a light hand on Adam's shoulder. "Thank you for helpin' her," she said softly.

Adam snorted. "Don't thank me yet," he said. "There's still plenty of ways for this to go wrong."

She punched his arm. "Don't be such a pessimist." Candice smiled at him and turned back to what little work remained before the evening crowd arrived.

Adam was just about to take another sip of his bubbly water when the hunter felt it. One of them. He did not smell it coming, nor hear, feel, or even taste the approach on the wind. After so many years there was something, instinct perhaps, but the hunter knew it was something more. It was a sensation beyond any of the physical five. A new sense was slowly created and refined over countless scenes of violence and tense horror. A warrior learned to sense the enemy, or a warrior did not survive.

After so long fighting, hunting, suffering… there could be no doubt it was one of them. He had known, from the moment he had forsaken his former life, they would come for him. He had made too many enemies, over too long a career; one of them would *have* to come for him. And in renouncing his former life, Adam had lost the protection that life had brought. All his enemies, all those that had suffered or lost or been humiliated by the hunter would eventually learn what had happened to him. And then they would come.

But why now dammit!?!

The door to the Waystation opened and he entered. Candice must have sensed something in Adam's reaction. Her friend had frozen, staring down at his glass. Adam did not blink, he barely breathed. Heavy footsteps approached the booth. Candice said nothing, staying frozen behind the bar. The figure stopped at the edge of

Adam's vision and stood waiting for an acknowledgment of his presence.

Adam grimaced and slowly raised his eyes. He looked at the face and at once recognized this one. "Hello, Simkiel."

Simkiel smiled down at Adam with perfect teeth. "Hello, old friend," he replied.

"We're not friends," the hunter growled.

"True, we were never friends." Simkiel took off the silk coat he wore and hung it up on one of the brass hooks attached to each booth. He then slid across from Adam without asking and slightly pulled up the long sleeves of his designer shirt. "I think that might be because, in truth, we were all a little bit afraid of you."

Adam said nothing; he just stared daggers and remained tense.

"All that violence you did," Simkiel mused. He steepled his well-manicured hands. "All those you slaughtered without question." He looked at Adam through his long, blonde eyelashes, lashes that matched his perfectly-coifed hair. "And, of course, all those you sent hurtling into the Pit." Simkiel titled his head slightly. "You never showed any remorse in your duties, any hesitation. You truly were a force of destruction." He smiled, spreading his hands across the stained table. "You *were*. And now you are here. Here you are helping another little girl. What happened, did you have a change of heart? Did you forget about that girl who died? Did you get tired of trying to destroy that body of yours?"

"What do you want, Simkiel?"

"I want you do die," he replied simply. "I want you to suffer, to feel the pain you, yourself, have inflicted upon so many of us, and then I want you to die and take your long overdue trip into the Pit."

Adam put his hands flat on the table. "If that's what you want, then let's just get this over with."

Simkiel smiled, lifting Holly's drink and curiously sniffing it. "You never were that bright," he noted, placing the half-empty glass back on the stained table. "*I'm* not going to do anything to you. Have you forgotten the rules already? Free Will. The ultimate sanction against us. Despite your crimes, Adam Kadmon is mortal, and thus entitled to Free Will. Therefore, it is up to another mortal to see you off this world."

"If all you can do is talk, then what's the point of this?"

Again, Simkiel smiled. "I remember you being so clever," he marveled. "How is it that you hunted down so many of us?" He stared soulless eyes at Adam. "I'm only here to distract you."

Adam started. "Distract me? Distract me from…?" His eyes widened and he leapt from the booth, sprinting for the bathrooms.

The door marked for women was open; the room itself was empty with signs of a brief struggle. Additionally, the rear door was open, leading into an alley beyond. Adam cursed himself for his arrogance and burst through the door, knocking the aging wood nearly off its rusted hinges. Standing in the narrow alley, with piles of garbage crawling along the walls, the hunter searched for a target.

At the far end of the alley a windowless white van sat with its side door open. Its engine rumbled eagerly as a pair of men lifted Holly's limp body towards the waiting darkness. Each was wearing some variation of a cheap business suit, with off-the-rack sportscoat and polyester tie in defiance of the early evening's oppressive heat. They were not masked, yet none of their faces was remarkable. Weapons of various kinds poked out from pockets and improvised holsters. A bottle of some clear liquid was in one's hand, as was a damp cloth only now being removed from Holly's blank face.

The hunter roared in fury, grabbing a piece of broken wood, and charging down the alley. He hurled his weapon with deadly accuracy, impacting one of the two men in the head, the one holding the bottle and cloth. The target spun to the ground in a shower of blood, the side of his head now sunken in from the impact. Flying less than a second behind the first missile was the hunter's knife, leaping with equal purpose into the second man's neck. He fell in the same moment as his comrade.

"Shit!" the driver called. "It's *him*!!!"

A third target appeared from inside the darkness of the van, this one with a gun in his hand. By then the hunter was there, grabbing the gunman's arm and pulling him from the safety of the van. A fist driven into the face should have ended the threat, but the fanatic had purpose and continued to fight. He pulled the knife free from his dead comrade's neck and plunged it into Adam's side, pushing at him but unable to penetrate the white leather coat. The hunter grunted and was forced back, allowing the fanatic to regain his feet. The two opponents faced each other, the fanatic clearly surprised to see no blood or even a sign of damage on Adam's white leather coat where he had stabbed a moment ago. That instant of confusion, when the eyes had turned away, provided the hunter all the distraction he needed; darting in, he grabbed his enemy's arm, stripped the knife away and spun, slashing the fanatic across the throat.

"For *her*!" the driver barked with raised pistol and fired.

The hunter reacted without hesitation, raising his arm and spinning. An impact caught his left shoulder and sent him flying against the alley wall with horrible force. Stars burst into his vision and the breath fled his lungs. Sounds of movement and the screeching of tires filled Adam's ears. His vision cleared in time to reveal his failure.

The van sped away, beyond any chance for Adam to catch.

Picking himself up, ignoring the shrikes of protest from injuries new and old, Adam turned back down the alley. They had taken their dead and wounded, preventing him any chance of interrogation. Adam stood alone for a moment, deciding on his next course of action. He absently wiped away blood from a new cut above his brow and reentered the Waystation. With absolutely no surprise, Adam found Simkiel still sitting at the booth, idly sipping at Holly's drink. "Where did they take her?" he demanded, storming up to the creature.

Simiel glanced dismissively up at the man. "Why would I tell you that?" he asked curiously.

Adam leaned in and put his fist on the table. "Because if you don't, I swear I'll purge you right here, right now."

Simiel smiled. "Try."

"Last chance," Adam snarled.

Simiel waited.

The hunter grabbed the smug bastard by the throat, fully intent on sending him straight down to the dark place. In a blur, the side of Adam's head was slammed into the table and his arm was wrenched, painfully, away from its socket.

"Like I said," Simkiel whispered into Adam's ear, "we were afraid of you… *once*. But this… this Adam Kadmon is nothing. This being you have become is no threat to me or any of the Chorus anymore. You have Free Will, but the moment you try to attack one of us, you lose that protection. Consider this your only warning and a lesson in reality."

Simkiel released Adam, who collapsed to the floor. A perfect circle of soft white light surrounded Simkiel's head, growing gradually brighter. "We tolerate your existence because there is always the possibility of redemption," he said. "But do not mistake my obedience to the Word for my personal desires."

Adam noticed Candice reaching under the bar and waved her off with a shake of his head. There was no need for her to die, shooting at something that did not bleed. He then looked back up at the Angel. "I'm still waiting for you to tell me where she is," he grumbled through the pain.

Simkiel shook his head. "You took on this task. See it through yourself. If this girl dies the same as the last one, it will be your failure… again. Do not blame us."

He was gone.

Candice ran over in concern. "What happened?" she asked.

Adam looked up at her in resignation. Of course she did not remember the encounter. Most people could not retain the memory of an Angel. For the bartender, Adam had been sitting and then was suddenly on the floor. "It's a long story," he grumbled, letting her help him up. "And there's no time."

She held a wet cloth to his temple, cleaning away the blood. "What're you going to do?"

The hunter narrowed his eyes. "Get answers."

10

*L*ilith Aubrey and her two guards emerged from her private elevator within the Meropis Building into the dark, cold interior of the private, executive parking lot. The low heels of her tastefully understated shoes sent long echoes through the nearly empty garage as she made her usual inspection. One of the large, well-dressed guards who accompanied Agarés' local ruler held a small tablet in his hands, inputting the comments his mistress made as they casually, but efficiently, circled the level reserved for Aubrey's senior-most lieutenants. Even in the dim lighting of the underground garage, she easily read the name plates attached to the walls above each empty space, indicative of those people who had put their families or personal pursuits above their duty to her.

Aubrey stopped at a particular empty space, only a few spots from her own. "How many times has Ms. Hollman failed to work late?" she inquired.

The guard holding the tablet pulled up the relevant records. "Several," he replied. "Most, actually."

"Would the question be better formed as: 'how many times as Ms. Hollman *ever* worked late?'"

The guard grimaced. He had heard of many punishments that began with such a conversation. "Yes, ma'am," he said. "You've never made a note of Ms. Hollman working late. She arrives on time, works the established hours, and then leaves."

"But puts in no additional effort," Aubrey concluded. She glanced back up to the posted nameplate. "Not the best example from my *former* assistant."

With the nightly inspection concluded, Aubrey turned and moved to her car. "Ensure that the Response Team is prepared for tomorrow night," she ordered, "just in case."

Her second guard nodded. "Yes, ma'am."

Having reached her own car, the executive held her hand out for the keys and silently began a count for how long it took her servant to deliver them. "Mr. Kadmon still has time to give me his decision, and I anticipate a positive one, but I want to be ready for any eventuality." Aubrey continued to stand at the door to her locked vehicle with hand raised, waiting. In the reflection of the window, she could see the guard behind her fumbling with his tablet, obviously having forgotten in which pocket he had placed his mistress' keys. The second guard, to his credit, did not give any overt reaction to his partner's distress.

Even better, he does not offer to help.

Stopping her count at forty-five seconds, the executive turned. She looked at her guard with a stern expression. "Is there a problem, Mr. Hernandez?" she asked without the slightest emotion in her voice.

"I'm sorry ma'am." To the man's credit, he maintained his composure in the face of imminent, and obviously justified, punishment. Finally, the fool recovered Aubrey's keys and presented them.

The imperial employer did not accept. "Mr. Hernandez," she said frostily. "I had exactly one hour to have my dinner and return. That time allowed me to make another meeting I have this evening before other business must occupy my full attention. Because of your incompetence, I am now late. Additionally, I must waste additional time correcting you. I certainly cannot delay my meeting or my business later this evening, thus the only item on my evening's schedule with any flexibility is a relaxing dinner. You have cost me those few minutes of recreation, Mr. Hernandez."

The guard lowered his outstretched hand and adopted a submissive posture. "I apologize ma'am. I promise that it will never happen again and can only hope that you give me the opportunity to regain any confidence you have lost."

Aubrey considered various possibilities. "As a member of my security detail, your performance thus far has been… satisfactory. However, in promoting you to my personal attendant, perhaps I made a mistake. You are not ready to anticipate my every need.

Perhaps you would prefer to spend your time like the other men in Security? Standard hours and home in time for dinner with your family?"

Hernandez continued to keep his eyes downcast. "No ma'am. I feel I can best serve Agarés here, serving you. I can best take care of my wife and daughter by trying to best serve you."

The barest hint of a sensuous, almost irreligious smile curled a corner of Aubrey's lip. Her eyebrow raised and her eyelids lowered slightly. "Very well," she said in a deeper voice. She ran an idle hand along the guard's chest. "I will give you a chance to redeem yourself."

The second guard stiffened and let out a gasp of surprise and pain. Aubrey turned in annoyance but gasped as a small spurt of blood shot from the man's mouth, spraying her face. The dying guard suddenly stumbled forward, into Aubrey, sending them both crashing to the floor. Hernandez, useless again, stared like the open-mounted idiot he was.

Adam Kadmon lunged for the incompetent guard while Aubrey struggled to untangle herself from the dead weight pressing down upon her. Throwing his shoulder into the worthless guard's middle, Kadmon pushed him back with terrific force, slamming her ex-guard into the nearby wall. The grizzled man then jabbed twice with his knife and, twisting with the same motions, puncturing both of the fool's lungs and letting the dying meat collapse to the concrete ground. Having finished with the distractions, Kadmon turned to Aubrey.

She had just managed to push the dead man off her and was pulling a gun free from his coat. Before she could even release the weapon's safety, though, Kadmon was there, twisting her wrist and stripping the gun from her hand, tossing it away.

Why the hell was the safety on? I'll have to reprimand Security.

With his other hand, now free of the knife, the beastly man grabbed Aubrey by the throat and picked her up from the ground, suspending her smaller body in the air with only a single, muscled arm. "Ninety seconds for security to get here," he growled, his hate reverberating down his arm and through Aubrey's entire body. "Think what I can do to you."

She lashed out with a foot, striking him in the groin. Kadmon grunted and dropped Aubrey, more than a little surprised by the attack. She hit the ground but stayed on her feet and leapt back, kicking her designer shoes free and deliberately ripping the hem of her tailored skirt in the process. She did not hesitate, appraising the situation instantly, and turned to run. She was no physical match for this savage man, especially when he was so enraged. Aubrey sprinted around her car as fast as her legs could carry her, moving towards the potential safety of the distant door marked exit.

Kadmon rolled over the hood of Aubrey's car and, with only a few powerful steps, hurled himself at her with a heart-gripping roar. His white leather coat flared out and the hunter caught his prey by the back of her collar, pulling. Aubrey drove her elbow into his stomach before snapping her forearm down, driving her fist into his large groin and turning to lash out with the heel of her palm towards his battered face. Kadmon caught the strike and twisted her wrist, driving his stony fist into her delicate stomach with terrific force. The woman was doubled over with his blow, so he grabbed the back of her coat and threw her at a luxury car, where she landed hard on the large hood, exposed and breathless. He then moved in, radiating his eagerness.

Aubrey waited, absently wiping some blood from her lip and watched his approach. Once close enough, Kadmon reached forward and she struck, using the hood of the bright red car to leverage a high kick. Kadmon's head snapped back from the attack, blood shooting from his nose. Instead of being humbled by Aubrey's expert strike, the bulging man only spun to the side, heedless of any pain, and grabbed her exposed leg. The great hunter pulled Aubrey up off the hood and drove his fist into the small of her back. Simultaneously, the warrior pushed her into the attack with a hand on her chest. Aubrey's arms flailed out, but she recovered quickly, grabbing Kadmon's wrist, ducking under the arm, and twisting it behind his back, trying to leverage him into submission. Instead the fighter braced his powerful legs against the now-heavily dented car and thrust back, shoving Aubrey against her own car with enough force to dent the door. She gasped in pain and disorientation as the world spun and the pavement reached up to catch her.

Without hesitating, the powerful man, the heat of his rage nearly boiling the air of the once-cool garage, grabbed his victim and rolled Aubrey onto her back. He then reached back with a fist and drove it down towards her face. In the last instant, Aubrey ducked away, letting Kadmon drive his punch into the concrete floor. Barking a curse, the beast jumped back. Aubrey regained her unsteady feet and pressed an offensive of her own. A blur of jabs, kicks, blocks, strikes, trips, throws, and recoveries followed. Neither combatant could achieve the immediate victory for which each was searching. Aubrey's dexterity and growing desperation countered Kadmon's advantages of power and skill. The many injuries that slowed him just a fraction of a second countered his far superior capability and experience, and Aubrey did not waste the minimal opportunities afforded her. The raging man soon abandoned his initial strategy and drew his knife again. Aubrey surprised him, though, when she pulled a pair of thick needles from the tight bun of hair knotted behind her head, letting a lustrous mane spill around her shoulders. Within moments, crimson decorated both combatants in a whirl of hair, blood, sinew, and hate.

Finally, Kadmon's greater experience won out. He feinted with his blade towards Aubrey's eyes, forcing her to raise both arms in defense. The strong hunter then grabbed her belt with his free hand and pulled, setting his shoulder into her stomach and flipping the shorter woman over his broad shoulders. In the same movement, as Aubrey was falling towards the ground, Kadmon sent himself and his elbow falling as well, directly on top of his opponent. A gasp followed the impact and she could not rise.

Heavy bootsteps at last announced the arrival of security. Her attacker picked Aubrey up and turned her so that she was facing her car, which placed the large piece of metal between the pair and the approaching guards. He then ripped open her blouse and tore free a long piece of silk, using it to bind her hands together in his iron-grip. Kicking her feet apart, Kadmon then pressed himself up against Aubrey's body and grabbed a handful of her long hair, pulling her head back. This forced the woman against her car and he against her. Together, they faced the approaching security team.

"Tell them to hold fire," he growled into her ear, the infernal heat of his icy rage searing her mind.

"Why?" she growled right back, struggling flutily against the man's great strength. "Do you really think I wouldn't hire men that could shoot well enough to shoot around me?"

"Maybe," he replied, breathing hate against her neck. Kadmon pressed even harder against Aubrey from behind, at the same time pulling back on her hair. "But do you really want to risk your life on that? How many of those men have you pissed on out there? How many of them might want payback? This could be a great chance."

Aubrey said nothing. She continued to struggle against Kadmon's unflinching grip but could find no purchase against his strength. Her arms were completely controlled by his hands and his grip on her hair was so powerful that she could not even twist her neck to spit in his face. She was helpless.

"Say it, damn you!" he growled again, almost biting the words as his growing fury thrust into Aubrey.

"Hold your fire!" she yelled through clenched teeth. "Hold your position and take aim, but DO NOT FIRE!"

"Fair enough," Kadmon conceded. "Now let's have a talk." He released his grip on her hair and hands. Before Aubrey could react, though, the hunter spun her around and pinned her against the car again. This time he put one hand around her throat. Where the other was, Aubrey had no idea, she could not tell over the pressure of his grip over her windpipe and the overwhelming power of his entire body pressed up against hers.

"Now," the hunter growled, his face only a breath from hers, "you answer. If you lie, if you say anything I don't like, I squeeze. Understand?"

Aubrey tried to nod but was again, unable to move against his strength.

"Say it!" he barked.

"I understand," she gasped, utterly in his power.

"Where did you take her?"

"What?"

Kadmon started to squeeze.

"Wait!" Aubrey choked. "Don't... un...der..."

He relented slightly. "Where did you take the girl?"

"Didn't! We had... deal! Waiting for... your answer!"

The man stared into her eyes. Finally, "Bullshit," he sneered and started to squeeze again.

"Swear," Aubrey gasped, her eyes rolling up into her head and her entire body trembling. "Wait-"

Kadmon relented, allowing her to breathe. "Let's say I believe you. Who else would take her?"

Aubrey took several ragged breathes, struggling to control herself. "Don't... know; could be... anyone, any... reason."

"Do you expect me to believe that it's a coincidence?" he demanded. Then he paused before saying, "This thing you're in contact with; how did you learn about it?"

When Aubrey refused to answer, the hunter began to squeeze again. Feeling the renewed pressure, she quickly obeyed. "Kiliahoté!" she gasped.

"What?" He allowed her air.

"The curator... Fort Burleson museum. Met him... fund-raising event... told me about... things."

"Where do I find him?"

"House... edge of town... Lives alone."

Kadmon was silent and still, staring hellfire into Aubrey's weakened soul. He leaned even closer to his captive, his entire body pressing against hers so that his barely-contained rage, his irresistible strength radiated through to her bared skin. He looked into her eyes with their faces separated by nothing but a wisp of his heavy, musky breath, and she felt pure terror at the sight of the unrelenting madness within. No, not madness... worse than madness, more powerful than madness... purpose. There was no fear in his gaze, no mercy, no humanity. She saw only destruction and death and... power. The hunter pressed his stubbled jaw against the woman's smooth skin as his breath steamed into her ear. She tensed, shuddering in fear and something else, something deep and primal. His hand remained locked around her throat and she remained helpless, something she had never felt before. "If I find out that you're lying to me," he rumbled into her ear and her fluttering soul, "you die. If the girl suffers because you wasted my time, you die. If you're setting me up, you die." He stopped then and drew away, just enough so that those nightmarish pools in place of eyes bored into her. "If the girl dies... You can't run from me; you can't hide from me."

Her legs, pressed on either side of his, trembled, all the strength surrendered. She would have fallen were he not holding her. Lilith believed him. Lilith feared him. Lilith had never feared anything, not even the thing with which she had made the deal, but she feared this... man.

Kadmon released her and walked away. The guards all raised their guns and took careful aim, a flurry of red dots concentrating on the man's chest. He did not pause in his long stride nor spare the guards the slightest glance.

"Let him go," Lilith said weakly. She weakly pulled her blouse together, trying to rise on unsteady legs. Failing this, she pulled herself up, leaning heavily on her damaged car. "One thing," the executive said to Kadmon in a voice she tried desperately to force into steadiness.

He paused and glanced back.

"I still want an answer... to my offer."

If Kadmon was surprised by her remark, he did not show it. Instead, he just shrugged with cold indifference to her. "I talked to the girl. She didn't have the chance to give an answer."

"Time's an issue," Lilith insisted. She released the torn remains of her blouse and instead tried to free her flushed face of the strands of her wild hair. The woman took a faltering step around the car towards the man, betraying her eagerness, her need. "You could have a place here, you know."

He raised an eyebrow. "What makes you think I'm interested in your... place?"

Her face flushed again, this time in anger. "You don't want me as an enemy."

"I don't want you at all." He turned away and continued up the ramp.

11

A call to the library quickly provided the address for a Joseph Kiliahoté. The mousey librarian who had, only earlier that day, aided Adam in another search, just as efficiently guided him again. Considering his target was the only Kiliahoté in Meropis County, Adam was confident that the librarian had located the correct address. Kiliahoté's house was typical upscale for that part of Texas. A low stone wall separated the large yard from the street. The one-story house had solar panels and was decorated in some cowboy throwback fashion. On getting closer, Adam fully expected to see either a Texas star or a cow skull decorating the gate. Instead, it had a stylized coyote.

Different, but still Old West décor, I guess.

Adam looked up at the nearly-full, ill-lit moon rising from the horizon. Holly was in the hands of dangerous people, operating on an uncertain timetable. Whatever ritual she had been taken for, it would happen soon. Different creatures demanded their ceremonies at separate times, but many had something to do with the moon. Adam stared hard at the heavy orb, feeling Holly's life race along with it. Every second Adam wasted on pointless encounters and dead-ends was one more the innocent girl was in danger.

Tomorrow it'll be full.

The moment Adam crossed the threshold of the open gate, the hair on the back of his neck stood on end. The hunter reached back and drew his blade, letting his eyes slowly take in the surroundings. A well-manicured lawn with a few sparse, decorative shrubs. A small aluminum toolshed in the far corner of the property, one door ajar. Cicadas giving way to crickets in their raucous celebrations of the early, midsummer evening. The dark house itself, windows open to take advantage of the evening breeze but doors and attached garage shut. Nothing overt demanded his attention and yet a powerful force had saturated this place all the way up to its threshold.

"Are you going to stand there all day or invite yourself inside?" a deep voice called out from the left.

Adam turned in place and half-raised his arm, ready to end any threat that appeared. As though he appeared from the night without warning, a middle-aged man stood behind and some distance to the side, next to one of the natural-gas lamps that adorned the gate. He had the typical dark skin and hair, well-groomed and lacking any weathering. He wore no jewelry nor carried any weapon. The man wore glasses and a dress shirt that matched his slacks and dress shoes, but no coat or tie in silent acknowledgement of the midsummer heat. He held a briefcase in one hand and his keys in the other, making an obvious effort to leave both in plain sight. Everything about this man said, *hey there, you can trust the friendly Indian.* Adam was not fooled.

"If you're planning to rob the place," the nice, simple Indian said in a friendly voice, deep with age, that perfectly matched his ordinary appearance, "I can come back."

"Are you Kiliahoté?"

"I guess that depends," he replied with a friendly grin. "Were you planning on killing him?"

"Not Plan A."

"So, what is?"

"You answer some questions and then I leave."

"And Plan B?"

"I *make* you answer some questions and then I leave."

"Well, if those are my choices," Kiliahoté motioned towards the front door. "Let's at least have a beer." He passed around Adam, who did not move, at a reasonable distance, keeping his hands in plain sight and the friendly smile on his lips. Following the man, Adam noted in passing that no car rested on the empty street, nor sign of departing transport.

The museum curator led his interrogator into the house. The inside was decorated much like the outside, with authentically-rustic furniture and a lot of earth tones. Native American artwork covered the walls from a number of the southern tribes, as did several bookshelves overflowing with books. Over the mantle of the dark fireplace hung a hand-drawn map of Texas from before even its time as a part of Spain, marking the territories of the various tribes that once held dominance. Adam took all this in and returned his knife to its sheath at the small of his back.

Kiliahoté went into the kitchen and returned with two unopened bottles of beer. He set one on a small end table and moved away. The older man then raised his beer. "To the quest for information," he said dryly and drank deeply. "So what information are you after?"

"Aubrey."

"Ah," the scholar turned and sat down in a large, leather chair that sat opposite the still-open door, motioning towards another seat across the room from his. "Why do I get the feeling this is about her… spiritual interests?"

"Look I don't have a lot of time here," Adam said. "You seem like a real nice guy, and normally I wouldn't want to mess you up, but for some reason, I'm trying to do the right thing here."

"You mean saving the girl's life?"

Adam froze.

"Maybe you should sit down," Kiliahoté suggested before taking another drink.

Adam sat and stared hard at the man.

Kiliahoté leaned back and took a breath. "Aubrey came to me, what, two or three months ago? It was right around the same time you showed up, actually. Funny how coincidences work, isn't it?" he chuckled into his beer. "Anyway, she tried real hard to make our meeting look like a coincidence but…" he shrugged. "She wanted to learn about the spirit world and how to make contact with something that could help her gain power.

"See," he continued, briefly setting down his beer to remove his dust-covered leather boots. "Aubrey already knew about certain things. Most of the executives at Agarés do. That place has a lot more secrets than you realize. But the problem with secrets is, if you tell them, they're not secrets anymore. So Aubrey needed to go outside the company for what she called, 'contact information.' I warned her that she wasn't ready for what she was asking, but she insisted."

"What did you give her?" Adam asked.

Kiliahoté shrugged. "Nothing she couldn't have gotten if she'd bothered doing a little research on her own. There are plenty of spirits out there eager to make a deal with someone desperate enough or foolish enough to risk their souls." The scholar glanced over at Adam. "Why don't you ask me what you really want to know?"

"Fine. Which one am I dealing with?"

Kiliahoté nodded, retrieving his beer and leaning into the seat with a sigh. "This one is pretty typical. It longs for some measure of the feelings it once had, the sensations. It can't experience the true joys of this world, of course. This particular Fallen spirit sees the joy that humans have through love and tries to fill the void in itself with what it perceives as love. For that, it craves virgin offerings. That's where your little friend comes in. Whoever sacrifices her to the Fallen's lust at one hour past midnight tomorrow will be granted the usual gifts of wealth, influence, and power. Of course, it's all just temporary and eventually, they'll have to feed the spirit again."

"Who else? Who else besides Aubrey had access? Who else wants the girl?"

"It's a group of them, actually. One of them was my assistant, a woman named Elise. She had access to all my research and used it to contact the spirit. She used it, or rather, *it* used *her* to gather a group of followers. They worshipped the spirit, making small offerings and earning small rewards. Eventually, though…"

"It wanted more," Adam finished. He had heard this story all too many times. He took the bottle and pried free the cap.

Kiliahoté nodded. "The spirit led Elise and her followers down a path of corruption. In just a few months, they were kidnapping people off the streets."

"This Elise? Does she have a last name?"

"MacAllister. Elise MacAllister."

Adam collapsed back into the leathery comfort of the chair. The cool detachment that he carried as armor around his unwanted soul crumbled as the name struck a nearly mortal blow. Elise MacAllister. Holly MacAllister. He collapsed into a nearby chair. "God," he whispered. "Her mother."

Kiliahoté nodded grimly.

"HER FUCKING MOTHER!?!" The beer bottle shattered in his hand.

Again, the scholar could only nod.

People taken off the streets. A husband and wife so horribly mutilated that identification of the bodies was impossible. An Agarés employee using his access to get vans for the abductions and equip cargo trucks with access to the military base, a place with plenty of secluded spots for their rituals. A Fallen Angel with a growing hunger for the ultimate sacrifice of pure blood. Holly.

Adam looked up at Kiliahoté. "You knew this was happening and did nothing?"

"I only found out recently," the scholar replied softly, looking down with a blank expression. "And by then it was too late. Truthfully, it never occurred to me that they would target their own child. I suppose it should have."

"Is there any chance I can get to them before they move her to the ritual site?"

"Maybe," he shrugged. "The sacrifice isn't until tomorrow night. They won't take her to their shrine until after sunset tomorrow. If you can find her before then, you have a chance. But the cult will already be gathering."

"How many?"

"Almost a hundred. They've all received many rewards; they're loyal to the death."

"I'll be happy to oblige. Where are they keeping her?"

The scholar shook his head. "I don't know," he replied. "None of my resources have been able to locate them; their shielded. Probably one of the gifts from the Fallen spirit."

"I can find them," the hunter replied grimly.

"Probably," Kiliahoté grinned.

Adam narrowed his eyes at the middle-aged man. A deep suspicion had been building in his mind and he needed it satisfied. "Why are you being so helpful to me?"

"You mean besides the threat of violence?"

"I think we both know you can defend yourself."

Kiliahoté leaned back with a look of innocence on his face. "I don't know what you mean. I'm just an historian."

Adam drew his blade and threw it at the nice, simple Indian in one fluid motion. His aim was perfect and there was no chance of missing. The weapon flew past Kiliahoté and struck the wall behind him. Adam had been aiming at the man's chest.

"Nice throw," Kiliahoté congratulated calmly.

"Who... *what* are you?"

"Someone who's trying to help you. Isn't that all that matters?"

"No. Something I've learned over the years: never trust free advice. Eventually, the bill comes due."

"Find the girl, stop Elise, and consider us even."

Adam shook his head. "That would be fine, but it still leaves one point unexplained."

"And what's that?"

"Why did you help Aubrey?"

"Oh yeah, Aubrey." Kiliahoté nodded, as though he had forgotten. "Well, believe it or not, she doesn't really have much to do with your immediate problem."

"I notice you didn't answer my question."

"I was hoping you wouldn't."

Adam just waited.

"I can wait longer," Kiliahoté warned. "You're the one on a timetable."

"Fine. But by not answering, you only ensure that I'll come back."

"Interesting point. How about this? So long as you don't ask *me* too many personal questions, I won't ask *you* the same."

"Puts me a disadvantage, since you know at least something about me."

Kiliahoté nodded sadly. "Yeah. I guess sometimes, it just sucks to be you."

"More than sometimes." Adam shook his head and stood, crossing the room to retrieve his blade before moving to the open door. "Keep in mind that you've stirred up a lot of chaos at Agarés by giving her that information," he said while he walked.

"You say that like it's a bad thing," Kiliahoté argued. "Agarés has done everything it can to impose order on this land. *Its* order. I think a little chaos is just what we need."

Adam turned at the front door and looked back at Kiliahoté with a dark, knowing smile. The scholar bit his lip, realizing he had said too much in front of someone with a great deal of experience in the supernatural. "Yeah," Adam said. "So, am I your new pet or just a moment's distraction?" He continued outside without an answer.

Kiliahoté followed, standing in his doorway. "You're a lot more than a moment's distraction," he called out as Adam reached the gate. "I know a chaos-bringer when I see one, and you are definitely what this town has needed."

Adam paused at the open gate. Turning back, the hunter glanced down at the stylized coyote wind and then back up at Kiliahoté. "I don't play games and I don't take well to tricks," he warned. "Remember what I used to do, what I used to be."

Kiliahoté smiled broadly. "How could I forget?" he laughed. "After all, Chaos and Destruction go so well together!"

12

The streets were dark as Adam made his way up Seventh Street towards the Balls n' Styx. The fading light of dusk had long since followed the sun down past the horizon, plunging Disanté's streets into a ghastly darkness the pregnant, ill-lit moon could do little to combat. The few working streetlights flickered erratically, painting the wide avenue in a demented yellow strobe that cast mad shadows against the stained and crumbling walls. The baleful midsummer breeze that had threateningly pushed against the decaying town had, with the retreat of the sun, gathered its strength. Brief, strong gusts of hot air flew angrily down the concrete veins of Disanté like the pulse of some raging, dying giant. This sent lifeless debris tumbling helplessly through the diseased canyon of Seventh Street. Adam continued on his course, heedless of the weather or what it contained.

The predators had long since crawled out of their diurnal lairs. Hungry eyes stared out at Adam as he walked up the street. Muttered growls floated out from the safety of the darkness; threatening and territorial, lying claim to some wretched corner of crumbling asphalt. From time to time one of the stronger beasts, a local alpha, would step forward from his pack and bark a challenge; but one glance from the hunter sent the curs back into the shadows. Many of them scurried after him, instinctively trailing in the wake of his rage like carrion-feeders; no doubt hoping for the scraps of whatever violence the hunter might bring to their urban wilderness. The scavengers knew better than to interrupt a true predator at his business, though.

Adam pulled open both front doors to the Balls n' Styx. The interior was packed with the assortment of evil one might expect once the hated sun was gone from the sky. Neon lights tried in vain to cut through the pall of think, noxious smoke, but could only produce a deathly pallor that shone off all the lost souls within. Thugs of every color and creed clustered around various gaming tables, yelling at each other in declarations of dominance. Precious metals and stones dangled from wrists, necks, and other body parts, reflecting the sickly neon glow. Clothing was loose and revealing, a riotous mixture of absurd style and seductive display. A large, glowing box played music that only added to the din of the crowd, mixing with an ambient noise that produced a chaotic dirge.

Adam took a deep breath, struggling against the hunter's instincts, and entered.

Delicious stopped him before Adam could take more than a few steps. "You gotta be out your damned mind to come back here!"

Adam stopped and looked up at the blob of a man. "How the Hell do you find underwear in your size?"

The enforcer's eyes widened and then narrowed in rage. "Mother-!" he balled up one of his massive fists and reached back.

"Really?" Adam asked with a raised eyebrow.

"What are you gonna do!?!" the enforcer demanded. He glanced around with his fist still raised. Several heads had turned their way and several hands had dipped low, going for weapons. "You a little outnumbered asshole."

"You only count as one."

"Delicious!" Junior's voice snapped out from the other side of the room.

The blob threatening Adam froze, his head snapping around. The music cut off instantly and all motion stopped. Junior stood in front of his office door looking angry. The local "businessman" still wore his expensive suit in defiance of the heat, complete with diamond tie stud and matching rings. Behind Junior, Adam saw a pair of men, both similarly dressed, moving to flank their employer.

"Do we have a problem?" Junior asked.

"No problem boss," Delicious hastily replied. "I was just dealing with this fool."

Junior leveled his gaze at Adam, a look that the hunter returned. The crime boss smiled and walked forward with a shake of his head. "Shit," he laughed, "more like you were about to get dealt with."

"I've got this," the blob objected.

"You've got what I tell you you've got."

Delicious took a step back and looked about uncertainly.

Junior stopped some distance from Adam, never losing his casual grin. "So, what brings you back?" he asked in a friendly tone. "Drink? Game? You're always welcome."

"Good to know," Adam replied evenly. "Talk."

The businessman nodded and gestured towards his office. "Right this way sir, right this way."

As Adam moved past, Junior directed one last hard look at Delicious before following his guest. The office was much cooler than the rest of the building, so much so that Adam's white leather coat brought a welcome warmth for once. Junior walked around behind a black metal desk, polished to mirror-brightness, and paused at a wet bar that held a full set of crystal. "Drink?" he asked.

"Pass." The hunter glanced back as the two gentlemen wearing the nice clothes solidly closed the office door and took up positions behind and on either side of Adam.

"Suit yourself," Junior shrugged. He poured himself a glass and sat down on his solid metal chair, gesturing for Adam to the same in one positioned on the opposite side of the obsidian-like desk.

Sitting, Adam cleared his throat. "You lied to me Junior."

"What?" he replied in a mockery of shock and offense. "I *lied*? How so?"

Adam steepled his hands over his stomach and continued. "I asked you today if you knew anything about the break-in at the MacAllister place and you said no. You also told me that you knew nothing about the kidnappings around town."

"All true," he replied with a shrug.

"Yeah, but some things have happened today that make me question your sincerity."

"Do tell."

"One, the group that keeps abducting people is using quite a bit of firepower. The kind of guns that are hard to bring in unless you have a contact."

"Well, there is a strong criminal element in this city," the criminal replied with a sad shake of his head.

"Two, I can now be reasonably certain that Agarés isn't the one bringing in the guns." Adam leveled his gaze at Junior. "You have the resources to bring in guns, though, and you would do all of it for a price without asking questions."

"A man has to make a living," he shrugged.

The hunter leaned forward in the chair. In response, Junior's guards took a half step forward but their employer shook his head. Forcing down a cold fury, Adam said, "So, here's what you and I are going to do: you are going to tell me where I can find this cult. You are going to do this right now, without any of your bullshit. I am going to use this information to hunt them down and kill most... probably all of them, and save the life of an innocent girl. I am also *not* going to break you into little pieces, do the same to your buddies behind me, and then go to work on this shithole business of yours."

He leaned in even further, letting the hunter speak. "Because I swear to God, any harm to that girl because you delayed my rescuing her, I will return on you threefold." Adam leaned back in the chair, waiting for an answer.

A few heartbeats passed before Junior replied. He smiled, waving his hands in surrender. "Hey, why wouldn't I want to help a nice guy like you?" he asked. The criminal leaned forward, writing an address on a slip of paper. "I do recall some business with people that just might be the ones you're looking for. All deliveries went to this place." He held up the paper. "It might be worth a look around."

Adam stood and accepted the address. Glancing down he nodded. "In the future, when you come across some information you think I might need, it would be best for you to just pass it along." He turned to leave.

"Nothing's free in life," Junior called after.

Adam paused at the door, glancing back. "How much is your life worth?"

The criminal shook his head. "That threat won't last. Sure, you could cause some damage but I've got guns and I've got people. I can find you. Is it worth going to war with me?"

Adam considered. "Fair enough. As long as you keep your business away from my attention, I promise not to go out of my way to cause you problems."

"How do I know what will get your attention?"

"Just be careful Junior," Adam advised as he walked away. "Just be careful."

13

$\mathcal{T}$he first guard died without a sound. The hunter caught him from behind and opened his throat in less than a second. The arteries on either side of the man's neck sent out a torrent of blood, spraying a relative cool in comparison to the heat of the Central Texas night onto the ground in front of them. The hunter held his first target tightly for the few moments of thrashing, taking care that the dying man could not reach for the weapon stashed in the small of his back or worse, the phone. Within moments, the twitching faded, and the hunter guided the body to the ground.

The now-dead guard had no radio. He and his fellows patrolled alone, out of sight from one-another. There were security cameras, but not with overlapping fields of view. The windows did not appear to be wired with detection or alarm systems. The hunter did not, could not, process this information in rational terms. His mind could not function like that; everything now was instinct. Adam was losing himself to the skills, the violence and destruction, that had caused his Fall. Worst of all, the flickering candle of his unwanted soul did not particularly care. This renewed feeling of purpose, of drive and the singularity of intent, was a welcome relief after months of self-loathing. Offering no consideration for the meat that had, moments before, been a man, the hunter dragged the body into a stack of old cardboard and covered it as much as was necessary before moving to his next target.

This one was no more aware of his surroundings than had been the first. Her head spent most time down, or up, lost in thoughts besides security, absently tapping on one of the tiny black boxes humans found so fascinating. One hand, not occupied with distracting technology, was stuck into a pocket, further reducing reaction time. This guard had two weapons, one in the back of her pants and one in an ankle holster. The hunter attacked from the front.

He waited at a corner of an alley, as silent as his old companion, Death. His breath came slowly and deeply. His body relaxed, but ready. He did not look out at the target but trusted his other senses. The sound of footsteps drew nearer, the light smell of perfume, and a pulse calling through the sticky air. His blade was ready.

One strike was all it took. His knife slid effortlessly into the target's lung with a twist. To be sure, the hunter grabbed the dying body and forced it against the alley wall, pulling his knife free through the side of the target's throat. Again, a few moments effort was all required to see the sentry safely dead and the body hidden.

One left.

This one was better than the others, which was why the hunter had left him for last. The third sentry walked with his hands at his sides, his eyes scanning the surroundings and his weapon tucked into a proper holster at the front of his belt for a fast cross-draw. This one would die the fastest to prevent trouble.

The hunter attacked from the rear. His knife entered the back of the target's skull at the base. Stillness and silence were immediate, and Death close behind.

The building was an old warehouse, long since fallen into disrepair. A burnt-out sign had faded with age and rust. The surrounding iron fence had several missing sections, and others that had fully succumbed to corrosion. Most of the high, multi-panel windows had at least some broken glass, those that retained any glass at all. The paint had once been red, but now, peeled and worn, made the entire building resemble a pock-marked, rotting corpse. Its only grace was the large surrounding parking lot and wide streets, empty buildings, and uncaring neighbors.

A pair of guards stood watch in front of the main doors. The hunter considered options in his almost feral way. Light peeked out from the inside, like half-blind eyes; so electricity operated within the building, making the emergency exit problematic. An alarm announcing his arrival would be far worse than any incidental scream of a doomed guard. Only a matter of time delayed the discovery of the missing sentries, so the hunter could not delay upon any entry through a doorway.

He moved silently though the heavy shadows, up to the side of a darkened corner of the warehouse. A drainage pipe rested against the corner of the building, rising to the roof. Two broken windows gaped within easy reach at the top of the drainpipe. The hunter began to climb. The weak metal softly creaked and groaned against his weight, but did not reveal his location to the ambivalent guards. He moved from one support ring to the next, carefully testing its security against the wall before hauling up on it and bypassing the few that felt too rebellious. In only a minute, he reached the windows above and grabbed the more fully exposed one on the right.

The hunter did not wait in the exposure of the window ledge, but pulled himself through and down, crouching on the rafters amidst the shadows within. A quick glance revealed a network of these support beams, granting him access around the entire structure. These were, in turn, riveted to several thick metal pillars spaced evenly through the large interior. The warehouse was vast and open, with large light fixtures hanging from the rafters at even intervals; most of these dead or dying.

The hunter waited for his eyes to adjust to the dim light while his other senses reached out for other sources of information. Several large metal containers, typically used for the shipping of goods between cities and continents, rested within. They sat, one on top of another, and bore the rusted evidence of long abandonment. Most of the containers bore the name and logo of Agarés, and most had doors that hung open. Divisions in the metal stacks formed hallways and banks of portable lights ran down the middle of these. Each light buzzed and flickered, casting a dull white light across the floor. The First Language, the same writing Holly had seen and described to Adam from her previous capture and escape, was scrawled in red and black across the occupied sections of the warehouse interior, spelling out prayers to a spirit of sensual pleasure and sinister generosity. This was a place of worship, then, dedicated to a Fallen Angel. There was no altar, nor other accoutrements of sacrifice; the cult seemed to be using this building only for holding victims before moving them to their holy site. The hunter continued his search.

The smell of coffee drifted up from the front of the building, where a small plastic window, open slightly, gave view to a meeting in progress. Voices, muted with distance but carrying emotion, called out to the hunter, their words a mixture of confusion and fear. He drifted along the rafters, drawing closer to the frightened voices, but remaining safely within the shadows.

"We should move the girl now," one voice insisted.

The hunter reached the wall separating the large interior and the low offices in the front of the warehouse. He crawled down a stack of containers, stopping on an uneven outcropping formed by an improperly-positioned stack. There, he waited, watching and listening.

A small knot of people, of varying races, genders, dress, and manner, were gathered in the one illuminated office. The only obvious quality they all shared was their age: they all seemed in late middle-age, greying though not yet withering. More First Language covered the walls, but that was the only oddity of the room. A coffeemaker cheerfully bubbled on a small metal table, sitting beside a box of pastries. A whiteboard leaned against a different wall, with a schedule detailed out, noting important times of kidnappings, tortures, orgies, and other company business. Several foldable metal chairs dotted the room, some occupied, some not. In all, the room had the sense not of the lair of an evil cult, but rather the meeting place of a support group. "The *Ímā* commands that the girl not be moved until tomorrow," another cultist objected.

"We know that the Fallen One is hunting us," a third person objected. "He's already killed many of our people. He may even find this place."

Murmurs of agreement accompanied the statement.

"We have used the words of our Lord," a woman declared. She was familiar to the hunter, though he could not pinpoint from where. She was of average height and unremarkable looks. Her clothes were expensive and she clearly spent a great deal of money on her appearance. She carried herself with more than self-assurance, but less than arrogance; she had the demeanor of someone desperate for respect but unsure of what to do with it. The hunter frowned and thought before the answer appeared: Isabel Hollman, Aubrey's personal assistant. "The power of the *Ímā* has shielded this place," she continued. "Nothing, not even God, can see into this place."

"This warehouse still isn't safe," another cultist insisted, this one dressed in the uniform of an Agarés guard. "We may be shielded from view, but the Fallen One can still enter. Only the shrine is protected by our Lord."

"Do you doubt the power of the *Ímā?*" Hollman demanded.

Silence followed.

"You all speak of the Fallen One in fear," she continued in a challenging voice. "So, you must doubt her power to stop him."

Mutters of objection.

Despite the hunter's almost overwhelming thirst for destruction, Adam believed he needed more information on this cult. The temptation to burst in and slaughter the entire group was almost overwhelming. But, if Holly was not in this warehouse, he would need to be able to follow further leads. Thus, despite the obvious targets below, Adam crouched in his shadowy corner and forced himself to wait and observe.

"We all believe in the *Imá*'s power," A man said, this one wearing casual slacks and a dress shirt, open at the throat. "It's natural to have doubts, especially in these difficult times, but these trials define our faith. Will you fall to fear or are you deserving of our Lord's gifts?"

The cultists murmured their agreement.

"Then go," the apparent-leader continued. "You know your duties. You know what must be done in preparation for tomorrow night. Remember, if the Fallen One comes upon you... we die for *her*."

"We die for *her*," they all chanted. All, Adam noted, except Isabel Hollman.

The group then broke up, with some gathering in a tight group within the office, and some leaving through the front door. Adam watched the interior door swing open and Hollman emerge from the office into the large storage area, accompanied by the man who had quieted the cultists' fears. The guy seemed familiar. Adam was sure he had never seen the man before, but there was something… He was of medium build, with a fair complexion and dark hair. He carried himself like a leader, but his eyes betrayed weakness; they shifted in all directions, from the darkness he clearly feared, to the woman beside him he clearly desired.

"That went well," Hollman said with a sly smile.

Her companion shrugged as they continued down the corridor. "Why must you always stir up trouble?" he demanded.

"It amuses me," she replied with a toss of her hair.

From above, Adam stalked them, moving silently along the rafters.

The man stopped and turned to face her. He glanced around to ensure the others were out of earshot, unaware of the predator watching from above. "There are better ways to amuse yourself," he said in a voice that deep with lust.

Hollman stepped in, pressing herself against him. Breathing deeply, she looked through long eyelashes at the man. "I do whatever I please," she half-moaned. "Just because you married the *Ímā* doesn't mean that I buy into your bullshit, you know."

Adam's eyes narrowed in suspicion. He looked harder at the man's features and mentally compared them to someone else he knew.

The man ran his hands along her body, almost without control. His breath came ragged as he leaned into her mouth, his face quivering with need. "Bitch," he snarled.

"Yeah," she groaned. "Too bad for you, huh?" Hollman shoved him back against a container door. She stepped against the opposite wall and leaned back, pulling up the hem of her business skirt. "Too bad there's no one else as sick as you are."

"Nobody's as sick as you are," he objected, walking forward.

"Definitely not your wife. Or your sweet little daughter."

The hunter's knife was in his hand as Adam fought against the cascade of revelatory information pounding against his mind.

The photo from Isandro's police file. Edward MacAllister. Husband of Elise MacAllister. Father of Holly MacAllister.

Dead man.

The hunter had his target. In the moment he was about to leap down and exact bloody vengeance, Adam regained control. Little would be served with such a confrontation. His priority was finding and freeing Holly. Only then could he deal with this scum. The hunter eased his tensed muscles and waited.

Hollman broke off their embrace, even as Edward MacAllister moved to open his clothes. "No," she ordered with a grin. "Not here."

"What?" he demanded. "Why? Where?"

She took several steps down the corridor, her smile turning vicious. "In front of *her*," she said. "It's bad enough I have to keep smiling at the *Ímā*, watching everyone kiss her ass. But treating your little brat like she was something special..." Hollman sneered. "I think it's time she had a lesson."

"What are you talking about?"

The woman ran a hand down between her legs. "In *front* of her."

MacAllister's face betrayed his shock. "Are you *insane*?" he chocked. "What the hell is the matter with you?"

"Think about it," she purred. "Think about taking me from behind and looking into her eyes. Running your hands down my body while she watches. Maybe she cries a little... at first." Hollman's hands ran all along her body, writhing in bliss at the thought of such depravity. "But maybe she can't help but watch... and *feel* something? Maybe she can't help... touching. Maybe... for Daddy?"

"You sick bitch!" he snarled through clenched teeth.

"How many times?" she asked, walking forward on swaying hips. "How many times have you whispered that name in my ear?" She leaned in to his ear. "How many times have you moaned it while fucking me? *Holly*."

The hunter shook with rage. Blood pounded in his ears and his grip on his blade was so tight that the fact it did not break was nothing less than a miracle. His breath, when it came, did so in a ragged snarl of hatred. Blood, pain, misery, and death filled his mind. Savagery beyond human capacity encompassed his soul as the hunter warred with Adam's desperate need to see his mission through.

This scum *will* die! But Holly will be safe first.

MacAllister grabbed his seductress by the arm and led her down the corridor, almost at a run. His eyes were unfocused, and his mind clearly lost to the fantasy Hollman had weaved. She did not resist their mad plunge forward, but only laughed at the man's weakness. Before long, they stood in front of a container door, undifferentiated from the others except for a few glyphs of the First Language scrawled on it, as MacAllister fumbled in his pockets. A key was produced and the door was opened.

"Go away!" Holly's voice called out in fear from the darkness within.

The hunter fell upon the two monsters, slamming them into the containers on either side of the door. Not content with that minor violence, he grabbed both by their hair and hauled backwards, throwing them into the wall on the opposite end of the corridor. They each hit, rebounding onto the floor, and fell away from one other. Hollman looked back and recognized their attacker with widened eyes. Without a thought to her companion, she fled.

The hunter did not care; all his rage was directed upon MacAllister. He stepped forward, snarling and fuming. The mewling, simpering sinner crawled away on his back, blubbering for mercy.

Mercy was not possible, however. The hunter reached down and picked his target up by the throat, slamming him repeatedly into the metal wall. He grabbed the sinner's face in a clawed hand and dug his fingers deep into vulnerable points, bringing gargled gasps of agony.

"Pain!" the hunter both promised and demanded.

"There!" Hollman shouted.

Adam turned. Hollman had returned with two guards. All three had guns leveled. Although the men hesitated, unsure of their aim given how close the hunter was to MacAllister, Hollman did not flinch. She fired, catching their enemy across the back of the shoulders.

The force of the impact, although it could not penetrate his white leather coat, still spun him. The hunter used it to turn and throw MacAllister towards them. Ignoring the pain burning in his back, he leapt into the small container in which Holly had been held.

"It's about fucking time!" she snapped.

"You're welcome." Adam scrambled along the floor to where the girl was chained. Still wearing the grey skirt and blouse she had worn to the Waystation that afternoon, Holly had been restrained at the wrists, ankles, and waist by a series of chains that were attached to the floor of the storage container. "I thought your uncle taught you how to get out of restraints?"

A guard appeared at the door. "Freeze!" The hunter threw his knife into the fool's eye without looking.

"Are you kidding me?" Holly held up the thick, elaborate chains. "Get me outta here, you ass!"

"Jesus, always excuses with your generation. Hang on." Adam darted back to the door and, acting quickly to try to avoid the worst of the spray of bullets erupting at his sudden appearance, grabbed at the dead guy. "Here," he said, handing the pistol over to Holly.

"What the hell am I supposed to do with this?" she demanded, holding the pistol in bound hands.

"I thought teenagers loved violent video games."

"Why don't *you* use it!?!"

Adam grabbed the chain binding her to the floor. "My hands are full." He started pulling. "And... I... can't... shoot... for... shit..." he snarled, straining against the squealing metal.

"How can you not shoot a gun? You're, like, a badass. Isn't there some rule that you *have* to know how to shoot?"

"Would… you… shut… the… FUCK… UP!?!" The chain bent and twisted, squealing against Adam's great strength.

"I'm just saying, how, in this day and age, can someone in your line of work…"

Adam roared in frustration as the chain snapped. He looked with satisfaction at Holly, fully expecting a gesture of gratitude. Instead, she just held up her still-manacled wrists and gave them a little shake.

Bullets snapped out from the door, striking Adam in the back. He barked in pain but did not move away, instead shielding Holly by spreading his white leather jacket wide.

"Kill him!" Hollman screeched. "Kill him!"

The hunter half turned the moment the shots paused, intent on ripping the cultists apart with his bare hands, but Holly beat him to the kill. Bullets shot out, killing the man at the door and forcing Hollman away in search of more underlings. Adam looked back at the girl he was supposed to be saving. "Huh," he noted.

"My uncle taught me some other things," she noted, her wide eyes betraying her steady hands.

"Next time, *before* they shoot me."

She just stuck out her tongue.

Adam finished breaking Holly's chains and then moved to the corner of her improvised cell. Motioning her for silence, taking a second to gently push the barrel of her gun away from his face, he then risked a quick glance out into the corridor. "Alright, it looks clear. Stay close and don't shoot me. I'm probably going to be killing people, so don't freeze."

"I'm ready."

Adam took a deep breath.

The pair moved into the corridor, staying close to the wall of storage containers. Total silence filled the warehouse. No movement, no threat.

Shit.

Shots rang out all around them. Adam wrapped his white leather coat around Holly as the pair retreated from the concentrated gunfire. As soon as they were too far to jump back into the relative safety of Holly's improvised cell, MacAllister and Hollman, along with more than a half-dozen cultists, appeared from around a corner, firing a variety of weapons. Adam moved them behind one of the large pillars that ran along the center of the warehouse.

"Get the girl!" MacAllister barked.

Two cultists appeared at the opposite end of the corridor, in the same direction that Adam and Holly were now facing, screaming and charging towards the pair. Adam threw his knife at one. The other reached them and ducked beneath Adam's quick jab.

Double-shit. A real fighter.

The cultist wrapped his arms around Adam's torso and heaved back, sending them both to the ground. A bullet struck near Adam's head. "Don't shoot at me!" he barked at Holly, still grappling, "Shoot at *them*!"

She did so, kneeling and firing with experience that belied her youth. Several cultists screamed and retreated, Holly's aim finding several targets. The reprieve was short, though, as her pistol clicked empty. Hearing this, the others advanced. Lacking his knife, Adam could not kill the cultist in his arms quickly enough. The moment he tried to let the fanatic go and charge back to Holly's side, the lunatic reengaged. Adam was forced to wrap his arms around the cultist's neck and twist, applying greater pressure until he heard the snap and the body went limp.

"Let me go, you assholes!" One of the cultists trying to manhandle Holly was writhing on the ground, the bleeding gashes on his face offering proof that she would not go easily or quietly. Three others, though, had picked her up and were now carrying her bodily back down the corridor, away from Adam. She lashed out with fists and feet, squirming against their grip. Again and again she landed blows on the men carrying her, but there were just too many.

"Holly!" he called out.

"Adam!" she screamed.

MacAllister, Hollman, and the remaining cultists fired more bullets, covering their retreat. This forced Adam back behind the column. He tried to move out from his cover, but shots nearly claimed his head the moment he did so. Helplessly he could do nothing as Hollman led the guards carrying Holly into the office. She was still struggling against her captors but could do little against so many. Adam tried desperately to calm his mind, to let the chill rage take over, but desperate fear for Holly's safety kept intruding on the hunter's calm.

Shit!

Shit, shit, shit, shit, SHIT!!!

Adam frantically looked around and then up. A fire extinguisher rested above his head; he grabbed it. Footsteps came from the corner in front of him. Adam turned and reacted a split second before the two cultists who were trying to flank him. He fired the extinguisher into their faces and then dropped to the floor, rolling through the resulting mist amidst their legs and towards the crumpled form of the first cultist he had killed with his knife. Blind shots rang out over his head until Adam reached the two men and collided with them. His knife flashed out in the dim light with expert, lethal skill, killing first one, then the other.

"I've got her!" Hollman called out. "Let's get the hell out of here!"

Adam put his knife away and grabbed the guns. He spotted Holly being dragged through the front office by Hollman and MacAllister. The last two cultists going with them were both oriented towards the mist that still covered Adam. He raised the guns and fired, sending a flurry of bullets flying out towards the guards.

His missiles hit all around the men, shattering glass, chipping concrete and wood, but did not hit either of them. It did force them to retreat and duck away from his frenzied attack. Dropping the spent and useless weapons, Adam drew his knife and threw it, implanting the blade into one cultist's neck. Seeing the second trying to reorient on him, Adam dropped onto the smooth floor and slid into the target's legs, collapsing them both into a confusion of limbs. Adam quickly climbed behind the bastard and wrapped his arms around the cultist's neck, twisting and squeezing. Lacking the time for such a tactic, Adam waited only long enough to weaken his prey before standing, retrieving his knife, and finishing the kill.

Picking up the fresh guns, Adam headed for the door. Shots rang out the moment he appeared in the light. A moment's glance revealed Holly being forced into the same van as before, this time by Hollman and MacAllister. Another cultist stood ready, aiming a gun towards the building, covering their escape.

In seconds, they were all loaded into the vehicle and speeding away. Adam ran after, firing as best he could in hopes of disabling the van. His shots all missed. When the guns clicked empty, he threw them aside and kept running. He kept running long after the red lights of the van had disappeared. He ran until his lungs burned and his legs collapsed beneath him.

Kneeling in the street, the oppressive heat of tar and asphalt pressing against him from all directions, Adam felt despair. His mind struggled to find some direction but none appeared. He had failed.

There were no other possibilities. He had the chance to save her, and he had failed.

Adam raised his fists and roared in helpless, useless fury.

14

ime passed. How much time, Adam neither knew, nor cared.

He did not, could not process time nor any sensation other than the crushing, intimate nothing choking his unwanted soul. This emotional pit was not like that into which he had fallen over the past few months, nor the one into which he would fall upon his mortal death. He was no longer lost solely within a chasm of self-pity and self-loathing, locked in an endless cycle of remembered failures. Nor was he trapped in torturous self-immolation, punishing and being punished for his many heinous acts. Rather, he was now in some boundless limbo, a claustrophobic void that crushed his heart.

Many humans have speculated over the nature of Hell. Adam knew the truth, of course, having sent so many there and seen the Pit for himself. Damnation was not fire and torture; not only that, in any case. Hell was a separation. Even the loneliness, most isolated human still knew companionship; life was everywhere in this fallen world. Every human is created hearing a heartbeat, feeling warmth, sensing others. A mortal life is filled with the presence of other life. Adam had not understood, for these months of misery; he thought he had been alone. He thought he *wanted* to be alone. He had reveled in his banishment from his loved ones and companions. For all the loneliness he had felt, he now understood, he had not been alone.

Now, in this empty street, in a forgotten corner of a silent town, he understood.

He stayed, kneeling in the street, for a very long time. Finally, a hint of warm air pulled slightly at the edges of his white leather coat and his unkempt hair. Insects began buzzing about, sometimes landing on him, sometimes biting, before flying off again. The growing, yet still intermittent wind set garbage flowing through the streets before settling randomly for its own slumber, awaiting the aid of the day to continue. Traffic on the distant highway began to drone a warning of the work to come. From behind rumbling clouds, the ill-lit moon, swollen nearly to full, continued her relentless slide towards the horizon. The world did not care about his failure.

As though from nowhere, hot rain erupted from the dark sky. Though unaware at first, Adam began to feel the unwelcome, searing baptism. The drops bounced off his white leather coat with little affect. They soaked into his hair, rolling down the back of his bent neck, adding to his sweat. The rain did nothing to cool the air, but did ease the awful pressure of the midsummer night, as though the world could finally weep, and was relieved with the sobbing. This feeble shower could not wash away either the blood or the doom that clung to him, but rather made the evidence of his impotent violence a burning anointment that painted crimson streaks down his face.

The rain brought with it remembered breath. Deep, gasping inhalations forced themselves down into Adam's chest, threatening a surrender to sorrow. He reached out for the hunter's calm, his uncaring rage that had so often protected him through the countless years of death and destruction. The hunter was not there, though. Adam was truly alone, abandoned even by icy protection against compassion. He battled now, not against cultists or corrupt humanity, not against Angels or Fallen spirits, but against a sobbing flood he feared he would survive.

Only once before had he ever felt so totally without worth. In all the missions over all the endless, blood-soaked years, only once did he ever, truly fail like this. Before that terrible day, he had been unconquerable; a destructive, undeniable force of nature. Defeat had been unthinkable and failure laughable. He had given no thought to the innocents caught in the wake of his destruction, so sure was he in his purpose. Holly had brought back some shadow of that surety; he was once again a righteous warrior. Once again, he had battled. Once again, he had failed.

Adam had no memory of standing, nor of choosing a direction, lost as he was in the shadows of his past. So many faces, little more than gaping mouths, moaned in hollow supplication as he shuffled through the empty, weeping streets of Disanté. The shadows of his victims looked on as the humbled warrior moved past. He could hear their whispers, still begging after all this time for a mercy he had never shown. They reached out with inanimate limbs, pleading for redemption that was not his to give, begging for relief from his judgement. Their darkness bled into him, into the leaden soul forced upon him.

The blinking streetlights watched his march, just as his peers had. They had looked down after the revelation of his disgrace and demanded something he could not... would not provide. So many voices called out for the destruction of this destroyer, in memory of his innumerable acts. He had offered no testimony in his own defense that day, lost as he had been within his despair. Even those to whom he had once looked for guidance, for loyalty and love, only stared back in silence that day. The lights looked down as silently now as then. They judged a Fallen warrior in his moment of disgrace and need.

Adam moved away from his judges and his victims, into an urban darkness. Whether this movement was forced upon him or of his own choice, he was not sure. Gaping silence wrapped itself around this self-loathing soul. He fell upon hard asphalt, but he welcomed the pain; so long without sensation of any kind meant that even the concussion of the oily street offered him some reference. The pain offered his mind a focus other than his imminent damnation. There was nothing around him, no sign of life among the quiet buildings.

As he struggled to rise, Adam's mind struggled to make sense of itself. A flood of new sensations burned themselves into him, each an unwanted sea of information. He yearned for the serenity of his earlier, unthinking entropy. Adam felt the pain of his life, the harsh reality of this brutal world and the misery of his body. He perceived the awful loneliness of his soul.

God, please help me.

Rosy dawn was just peaking in the east, gently waving away the stormy night. As Adam walked into the tiny courtyard of his apartment complex, uncaring of the half-empty pool or the rotting stench of humanity, he was only vaguely aware of the clearing sky. He climbed the crumbling stairs and opened his front door, a blast of cool air from Holly's new air conditioner forcing away the furious regrets clawing at his hated soul.

The darkness inside was little problem; he was used to stumbling back from a night of drinking at the Waystation to collapse in his bed. He entered his home and closed the door, but tripped almost immediately. Swearing, he reached for whatever had caught his foot. Pulling it to the couch, Adam found one of the lamps Holly had insisted on buying and turned it on.

Her bag. He had tripped on her bag. She left it near the door before they had left for the Waystation. Adam stared at it blankly, as though it were some strange new animal. He leaned back on his clean couch, looking around his clean apartment. Pictures hung on his walls, curtains covered his window, appliances sat on his counter, and her bag sat on his table.

Adam stood and entered his bathroom. He ignored the riot of colors and smells scattered around. Instead, he stripped and showered. A moment of irritation flashed when he realized his small bar of soap was gone, replaced with some bottle full of slime. The instructions seemed simple however, and the coarse brush needed to apply the slime was refreshingly painful on his many wounds. The smell was not terrible.

His hand paused at the colorful towels that had replaced his simple brown one. Adam angrily ripped the soothingly blue thing off its rung and dried himself before letting the offensive towel drop to the floor.

Adam entered his bedroom and moved to the dresser, intending to retrieve the shorts he normally slept in. With little surprise, he noted several new articles of clothing. He angrily snatched a pair of shorts and put them on, reluctantly conceding their comfort. Adam was about to turn away when he spied something that brought him to a complete stop.

Sitting in the corner of the room, clearly intended to be hidden from casual sight, was a small bear. Adam leaned down with a grimace and picked it up. The small brown thing was as adorable as the toys were meant to be, attracting the adolescent girls who bought them. Its soft brown eyes were wide and looked up in supplication.

Adam sat on the edge of his bed, very gently holding the small gift.

She said she didn't leave the apartment.

She had told Adam that she convinced a neighbor boy to go shopping for her, retrieving items on a drawn-up list. Holding the small toy, he realized her lie. Any boy who would be convinced to do such a task through the flirtations of a half-naked girl would never think to buy something like this. She had left the apartment, at the very least to get this gift for him, and then lied to him about doing so.

Adam tried very hard to be angry at Holly. He reached desperately for some measure of the hunter's rage at her deception, her defiance, her foolish risk-taking. He sat on the edge of his bed, holding the absurd brown bear, and struggled to find the frozen center that had kept him sane for so long amidst so much horror, bloodshed, and destruction. Adam could not find his anger; for the first time he could remember in his long life, he could find no trace of the rage that had defined him.

Small drops of water fell onto the bear as it shook slightly in his grasp. Holly, the innocent Adam had sworn to defend, the girl he had promised no harm would touch, was in the hands of vile, disgusting, *things*. She was alone and scared. Again and again, he heard her voice, calling out his name from the darkness.

A line, barely a sliver, of light spilled over the bear. It slowly crossed the soft brown toy, now covered in small wet spots. Adam glanced over, towards his window and the source of the light. A beam was reaching out, though the separation between his new bedroom curtains. He looked through the minor obstruction and saw that dawn had at last arrived. The sun, peeking over the muddled urban horizon, had cast a single ray of light through his now-spotless window and onto the bear in his hands.

Adam glanced back down at the bear and then stood, moving towards the window. He threw open Holly's curtains. The sun had freed itself from the urban horizon and was beginning its climb. The warmth of this new day washed over him, warming him and filling him. Still holding the gift, he stood there, bathed in the radiating light. A new fire filled Adam's chest, spreading through his whole body. This was not the rage that had fueled him for so long, but it was very close. Breath filled his chest, not in choking gasps or sobs, nor in hissing pulses of regret. His mind cleared, and his vision sharpened. His chest filled and his vision cleared. Purpose returned to him; a single face filled his mind's eye, along with a promise he made that would *not* go unbroken, no matter the cost. Not this time.

He still heard her voice calling out, and he would answer.

Turning back to the darkness but keeping that new fire burning within him, Adam placed Holly's gift on his dresser. And then he got back to work.

15

*A*ubrey's phone picked up after the second ring. "What?" she demanded angrily, her voice thick with sleep.

"You have a traitor," Adam said calmly.

The woman's voice cleared. "Who?"

"Isabel Hollman; your assistant. She's with the cult, one of the leaders. They've been playing you."

"I'm aware of the implications!" she snapped. "Did you deal with her?"

"Escaped. I need a location."

"I'll handle it," Aubrey said firmly.

"No," Adam replied with even greater firmness. "I need information; you can have her after."

A few seconds ticked by. "Fine. I'll run a trace. You'll have a location within a half hour."

"Good. Once I've finished with her, I'll call you with a location to pick up what's left."

"Leave her alive," the executive insisted. "There are certain protocols when dealing with betrayal."

"Fine."

Adam was about to hang-up, but Aubrey called out. "Something else."

"Quickly."

She hesitated. More time passed. "What other updates do you have?" she finally asked.

"What?" he started. Adam glanced at the phone in confusion.

"Do not forget that I have a vested interest in this matter," Aubrey explained quickly. "I wish to remain informed."

"The status is they have Holly and I'm going to get her back."

"You let them get the girl!?!" she yelled.

"And I will get her back," he added firmly.

"How could you let them get the girl?" Aubrey demanded. "It would have been better to just shoot her!"

"I'm hanging up now."

"No! Fine! Just... explain."

"Aubrey, what the Hell is this?"

"What? I want to know what's going on."

"... Aubrey, are we chatting?"

The silence was telling. Finally, "Just... get her back you fool!" The line went dead.

Markland was only just beginning to respond to the emerging sun, spreading out to catch the early-morning rays. The tightly-clustered townhouses briefly opened windows to allow a moment of air not cooled by machine. Rows of luxury cars happily chirped to life, greeting their masters. Impeccably-dressed joggers scurried along perfectly-manicured trails. Well-groomed pets eagerly led their bored owners to those areas designated for natural functions. The sprinkler system automatically began spreading excess water onto flawless lawns, despite the heavy rain the previous night. The residents took little note of Adam as he moved through their haven, despite how obviously he did not match the surroundings.

Markland offered the citizens of Disanté, those who could afford to live safely within its borders, a welcome harbor from the chaos of their city. Only fine, upscale shops, restaurants, and other businesses catering to the affluent residents could be seen from the gated community. Parks and playgrounds, all kept pristine, dotted the wide streets. A scattering of trees, few native to Central Texas, lined the perimeter wall; all the better to deny any outsiders a glimpse within. City police actively patrolled Markland's exterior, while private security protected the interior. This granted the inhabitants a false sense of security, belied by the predator entering their garden.

Adam had little trouble penetrating the security. The hunter considered incapacitating the guards at the front, eagerly tempting Adam with a satisfying chance at violence. Just as quickly as the idea presented itself, however, he dismissed it as unnecessary. A side entrance, far away from the main streets, was open and in use. Several men, easily differentiated from the residents by their stained working clothes, weather-beaten skin, and general lack of entitled arrogance, were exiting the domain of their social superiors. Adam moved towards them.

Upon his approach, the group turned as one and eyed him wearily. Adam kept his hands free of his pockets and his face neutral. One of the men, older than the rest, stepped forward with a raised chin. Adam did not pause in his stride as he headed towards the man. Without a word, he reached into the side pocket of his white leather coat and removed a large roll of bills, handing the money to the leader of the laborers. The leader wordlessly took the money and a path opened for Adam.

Adam moved casually through the uniform streets. The neighborhood was arranged in a carefully-planned simulacrum of organic growth, with identically-curving streets running parallel to one-another, and each street having the same number of condominiums. Each building was identical to the others, consisting of two units with two floors. The streets, though named rather than numbered, were arranged alphabetically, and the addresses were aligned sequentially. Locating Hollman's home took only as much time as the walk.

The other unit in her building was silent. The occupants were either home and asleep or already departed. An older woman passed Adam in her vehicle as he approached, having pulled out of the shared car port, but remained oblivious to someone so beneath her status. Adam climbed the low steps leading to the condominium.

Hollman's door was open.

The hunter pulled gloves out of the pocket of his white leather coat, moving along the stucco wall beside the door. He heard a pair of voices within, although their words were too low to make out specific words. He paused outside the door, glancing around from the advantage of Hollman's porch but saw no signs of potential witnesses.

He burst into a short hallway, looking into the living room and slamming the half-open door into the wall as he did so. A pair of men started at his entrance. They were both taller than Adam, but not as large in the shoulder and dressed in similar clothing as the other residents of Markland. The hunter lunged at the one on the left, rolling over the intervening couch to come up in front of his shocked target. Grabbing the man, Adam rammed his knee into the target's stomach, spun in place, and pulled the man over his shoulder. A hard trip to the thick carpet and a kick to the chest put the man to sleep for later interrogation.

The second target turned towards the stairs. "He's here!" he shouted in panic.

His face, turning back towards the hunter, was greeted by a gloved fist. Adam grabbed him and shoved the man into a wall before grabbing the back of his head and slamming his face forward. The limp body smeared a bloody streak along the beige wall as it fell. Adam then moved to the stairs.

The hunter glanced as best he could up the squared-spiral, silently cursing the deep shadows. He cautiously moved up, hugging the wall, but stumbled back as gunshots rang out from above. The sounds of a rapid retreat and a slammed door suggested the stairs were now clear, so the hunter bounded up to the second floor.

A long hallway had three doors, two open. At the farthest end, one door was shut. The hunter moved forwards. He paused only briefly at each open doorway, confirming with a glance that the bathroom and disheveled boy's room were both empty. He then squared himself and kicked open the last door with great force.

"Shit!" Hollman cursed. She kept firing until her gun clicked empty. The hunter had anticipated this, and spun immediately after his kick into the boy's room until he heard the clicks. Adam entered a large, luxuriously-decorated bedroom and faced Hollman with a look that would chill Death herself.

Hollman, standing at the far side of the room, dropped her useless weapon and held her hands up. "Wait!" she yelled. "Just wait! We can talk!"

"Oh good," Adam said, slowly moving around the large bed. "Offer me a deal."

The terrified woman backed against the glass door leading out to her balcony. "Anything!" she swore. "Anything you want! Please!"

"You know what I want," he replied, still advancing. "You've got one chance." Adam drew his knife. "I'm not wasting any more time with you people. You tell me where she is, *right now*, or they will never find all the pieces of you."

Hollman's entire body trembled as she pressed it against the door. Her face had lost all color and tears ran freely down her face. And then her eyes flicked behind Adam.

Shit.

The hunter dived to the floor just as bullets raced past his head. Adam swore aloud as he rolled across the bed and against the now-open closet, tangling into the legs of the man that had been hiding there. Both men wrestled on the floor, grunting and snarling. The cultist tried lifting his legs, wrapping them around Adam's waist. In response, the hunter kicked his knees up and used the new leverage to stand, lifting the cultists with him. A look of terrified realization and anticipation flashed into the man's eyes in the same instant that the hunter dived forward. The thick carpeting could do little to cushion the cultist's landing, especially with Adam's bulk coming down on top. A small burst of blood from the man's mouth and his gargling breath told the hunter his opponent was incapacitated, so he stood and reoriented on Hollman.

The glass door was open and the light curtains drifted in the gentle morning breeze.

With a curse, the hunter charged forwards, raging at the sight of Hollman on the carport roof a short distance below, running away.

The hunter exploded through the window, the curtains flaring out like gossamer wings. Roaring in fury, he stormed across the roof of the carport after Hollman. She glanced behind once reaching the edge but did not hesitate, dropping out of Adam's line of sight. He continued his charge and leapt off the carport. Hitting the ground and rolling to his feet, Adam turned back, ready to continue the hunt.

Hollman's car charged at him.

The hunter leapt forward, onto the hood, jamming his knife into the metal and grabbing for whatever hold his free hand could find. He pulled himself forward, snarling his rage as Hollman twisted the vehicle first one way, then the other in her frantic attempt at escape. The woman screamed and sobbed as the hunter began to pull himself up towards the windshield.

Hollman turned her car from side to side, heedless of the screaming, cursing neighbors that she nearly ran down. She crashed through manicured shrubbery and exploded through fences, sending debris flying in every direction. Hollman tried desperately to either shake her attacker free or otherwise force him off the car. Her efforts only served to further enrage the hunter.

The swerving, increasingly-distressed vehicle squealed passed a security car that made no move to pursue or assist, its occupant no doubt weighing his small salary against the obvious danger. Similarly, the guards at the front gate took only the most minimal effort at waving the car to stop before diving out of the way, wanting to protect themselves more than the pampered residents under their charge.

The hunter pulled himself up, ignoring everything but his target. He reared up, leveraging against the knife imbedded in Hollman's hood and threw his fist against the windshield. In response, the safety glass splintered and warped, unable to resist the violence forced upon it. Hollman desperately barreled through the open gate, onto the large business street that bordered Markland, sending a chorus of protests from surrounding vehicles as they desperately tried to evade her.

A pair of police cruisers, forbidden from entered the neighborhood, had pulled onto the street in an attempt to block the rampage. Spinning the wheel as fast as possible, Hollman sent her car skidding into the improvised barricade, slamming her car against the police cruisers. The sudden crash caused such inertial force that the hunter was torn from the hood, spinning over top of the police cars, and crashing into the peace officers themselves. Hollman did not wait to discover his fate, though, but shot away, another series of horn blasts and profanity accompanying her departure.

Adam stood with a curse, intent on continuing the pursuit, but the cops grabbed at him. The hunter twisted one cop's arm and ducked under it, throwing his shoulder into the back of the first cop and forcing him into his partner. With an oath, the second cop stumbled back against one of the cruisers and reached to his belt, pulling free a stun gun. The hunter grabbed the man's wrist and adjusted the aim, letting the electric current instead hit the first cop. Using the second cop's confused horror at having tased his partner, the hunter grabbed that man and threw him to the ground, landing a kick to the cop's head and ending the fight.

Adam stumbled off the street, looking in the direction Hollman had driven and ignoring the scattering of onlookers, too busy pointing their phones at him to consider helping the police. His target was gone.

16

The area around Markland became increasingly congested with police and onlookers. With so many influential and affluent residents suddenly at risk, local law enforcement was, of course, eager to make a show of how active they were. Police cruisers patrolled the area, improvised roadblocks went up along the busier streets, and a great many uniforms were deployed to assure the disturbed residents back into their privileged apathy. Adam did not linger.

Because so much of the effort made by the Disanté police was oriented towards the appearance of effort, rather than actual effort, Adam was easily able to avoid detection. He had only to stick to side streets and alleys. This allowed him to travel well out of Markland's proximity without incident. He could not travel much further, however, before his damaged body's aching protests to his movement demanded attention.

Adam considered his options as he searched through a small pharmacy. He ignored the frightened stares and muted whispers from the handful of customers while retrieving alcohol, gauze, and a few other items. No doubt the sight of a filthy, disheveled, bloodied, and stinking man walking through a drugstore was surprising to the good people who lived close enough to Markland to share in some measure of its social propriety. A small child kept trying to call its mother's attention to the angry man as he passed by, but the frightened woman shushed the infant and hurriedly left the store. Adam's continuous muttering to himself as he snatched items from their shelves likely did not help.

There was no point in trying to pursue Hollman, Adam noted. She was now aware of being tracked. More importantly, the cult was aware of it. They would not allow her to lead the hunter to Holly.

Likely, the moment Hollman reported their encounter, Holly would be moved again to a location the woman knew nothing about, for fear that Adam would eventually be successful in capturing and interrogating Hollman. She was too great a security risk to remain informed, so she would no longer be informed. Adam could therefore waste no more time on her. The question remained as he approached the register as to how he was to find Holly. He needed to find someone that knew her location. After all the attacks the hunter had launched against the cult, they would be very paranoid, keeping her location known to only a very few. This would minimize the chance of Adam interrogating the right person. So, who would know? Those guarding her, obviously; this close to the ceremony, it would be foolish to change guards, so whoever was watching Holly was likely to remain doing so. Who did that leave? Only the cult leadership.

The wide-eyed, pimply boy behind the counter stared up at Adam as the hulking man deposited the medical supplies for purchase. "Will that be all?" he squeaked in fear and puberty.

Adam snatched a bottle of water from a nearby cooler and tore the cap off without expression. "Chapstick."

An older man with thinning hair bravely stepped forward. He wore a lab coat and walked with the surety that only came with either experience or the abuse of medications. "Why don't you take out the trash, Danny?"

Danny looked to his employer in gratitude and nodded, hurrying to the back of store.

The pharmacist placed his hands steadily on the counter in front of Adam. "How can I help you sir?" he asked carefully.

Adam twisted his neck until a loud pop echoed off the walls. "You can hurry the Hell up."

The pharmacist looked down at the supplies and reasoned their intent, made even more so by the dried blood caked onto his customer's battered face. "I'm only guessing," he said carefully, holding up the large bottle of nonprescription painkillers. "You have no interest in going to the free clinic?"

Adam reached into his coat pocket and pulled out a bundle of money, flipping one large denomination bill towards the man. "Still waiting for a price." He flipped another bill.

"These won't really help," he pointed out, indicating the pills after only a brief glance at the increasing amount of money being offered. "Perhaps I can recommend something more... efficient?"

Adam said nothing but only waited and flipped forward another large denomination bill.

The pharmacist moved back to the row of bottles secured behind the counter, waving away one of his younger assistants who was waiting and watching with a hand on a phone. The businessman returned in moments with an unmarked pill bottle and handed it over. Adam completed the transaction, collected his supplies, and left.

The local park a few blocks away offered a convenient place for Adam to tend to his wounds. Because so much of the city's money was concentrated in surrounding neighborhoods whose residents used the facility, it was well maintained. Thus, the small public bathroom offered a functional place for a little combat care. The only disadvantage lay in the abundance of midmorning occupants to the park, mostly children and their minders. Privacy from this minor crowd was gained in the small public bathroom.

The distorted reflection from the bathroom mirror displayed an unencouraging sight. Adam's face was still unfamiliar, being as new as it was. Further, the past two days had inflicted so much damage that even given the chance to heal, the face showed a lot of wear. The huge gash across his forehead would scar, he grimaced while applying alcohol it. The broken nose he yanked back into place would likely remain crooked, matching the uneven lines that ran in odd places. Only his eyes held some hint of who he had once been; they held a glimmer of purpose that Adam had previously thought forever lost.

Removing his coat and shirt, Adam tended to his bruises. Even viewing his sides and back in the mirror, he marveled at the extent of the damage. Nearly his entire body was covered in discolorations. He could not tell where one patch of damage ended and the other began, and so treated his entire torso as one giant bruise. Adam grabbed the ointment from the bag and paused after opening the jar; the smell filled the small room, sending him back to the previous day. Try as he might, the hunter could not force away the memory of Holly tending to his wounds. Adam angrily dug his fingers into the jar and rubbed the offensive stuff onto his sore body, pressing with enough force to justify the tears that had formed.

Kiliahoté had said that Holly's mother was the leader of the cult. This thought centered itself in Adam's mind as he finished his work and dressed. What the hunter observed last night in the warehouse seemed to support that. Making assumptions about one's enemies could be dangerous, but considering the climbing sun and feeling the press of time's passage, Adam knew he had to start taking a few leaps. If Holly's parents were the leaders of the cult, or at least, in the leadership, it made sense they would know where she was or could find out. Conclusion: a conversation with either of Holly's parents would prove illuminating.

Besides, Dad needs killing anyway.

Just as Adam had pulled on his white leather coat and turned to leave, a uniformed cop entered the bathroom. The hunter stared at the startled patrolman for a second, weighing his options. Clearly, the witnesses outside Markland had transmitted his description to the police, a description supported by more reports from the good people of the pharmacy or the park.

"Alright buddy," the cop said with one hand raised and the other resting on his weapon. "Why don't we go for a ride and leave the nice people alone, huh?"

The hunter just stood there, preparing. Since leaving the scene of his battle with Hollman, Adam had been increasingly concerned that some bystander would alert the searching police of his movements. Stopping to tend his wounds had been a calculated risk, but one that he felt justified when weighed against trying to continue without doing something to tend to his damaged body. Clearly, he had been wrong.

Now I have to kill a cop.

"Come on now, friend," the patrolman said. "There's some good food for you at the shelter. You guys know you're not supposed to come into the park in the daytime, so why don't you just let me..."

"Ah shut up, you..." Adam pushed past, walked out muttering to himself and ignoring the ignorant cop's protests. "Damned stupid, ignorant, head up your ass, son of a..."

Adam left the park, muttering to himself a growling diatribe that continued for most of his trip to the MacAllister home.

The MacAllisters lived in one of the better neighborhoods of Disanté. While not as nice as Markland, nor as insulated from the rest of the city, the evenly-spaced houses still bore the signs of comfort reserved for those families who had extracted themselves from the common poverty increasingly present in world. The street was quiet and well kept, with evenly-spaced light posts and signs advising the many rules of civilized living. The named roads led down irregular cult-du-sacs, occasional shops, and other facilities to support the local families. The houses were similar but not uniform. Each home showed signs of individualization, with decorations in windows, small gardens, and even dogs barking from the safety of their fenced yards. Only the police barrier tape marking off the doors and windows of the MacAllister home marred the suburban perfection of the area.

Adam did not bother with subtlety. The police would still be busy comforting the distressed wealth of Markland to bother with any incidental calls from less influential homes. He tore the tape off the MacAllister doorframe and forced open the door. Inside was a chaotic mess. Picture frames were broken and scattered throughout the entry hall. Shards of glass crumbled at his feet as he closed the door and entered further. Several holes had been punched into the wall by something larger than a fist. Valuables were scattered down the hall along with large, open bags. Nothing appeared obviously missing.

Adam glanced in the dining room and adjoining kitchen but saw nothing noteworthy, just more of the overly-performative violence. Overturned cabinets matched the broken table and chairs. The darkened refrigerator had been left open and the food long since spoiled. Broken dishes joined with assorted cooking implements scattered around in an obvious display of wanton chaos.

The living room was the true show. The shredded furniture had been moved against the walls. The walls themselves were covered with First Language glyphs, preventing any Celestial observation. The heavy entertainment center had been overturned and dragged into the middle of the room. A tangle of knotted ropes still hung from the corners and spread across this improvised altar like a flowery bed in some twisted, nightmarish forest. Bits of cloth, flesh, and hair still clung to the metal and wood. Adam traced a light touch along the overturned entertainment center, sensing the dark entertainment for which it had been used. Distortions in the carpet showed where a second victim had tried to struggle against restraints. The whole room stank of lust and gore. Everywhere he turned his experienced eye, Adam saw evidence of a bloody bacchanal. What should have been a place of domestic contentment had instead been used as a stage of pain and horror.

Two victims, then. One had been held down on the entertainment center, stripped naked and slowly cut in the greatest number of places before death. The second forced to kneel and watch, probably also naked. The cult would have humiliated their victims for their own feelings of power. There would have been sex, of course. No blood sacrifice without an orgy, for some reason the hunter never understood. They would have mutilated the body of the first victim as the second watched. All the better to terrify. Then the cult would have tied the second, probably the female, on top of the first in a parody of lovemaking. Then would come the second round of cutting, sex, and mutilation.

In their pursuit of the rewards a Dark Angel could provide, worshippers were inevitably taken down paths to the worst part of human appetite. Adam picked up the fireplace poker in a gloved hand from where it had been lying on the floor. The police had left it behind, not understanding its use, but the hunter sensed its dark history. Stained, pitted, and still holding the stench of torture, the iron radiated the aftereffects of evil. Life as a human being meant being subjected to someone else's humiliation at some point, the hunter knew. People inevitably fantasized about retribution, although they would never act upon those fantasies. Worshipping a Dark Angel forced those darkest corners of the mind into expression. The creature's greatest temptation was not the gifts it offered, but the sin of permission. Because the Dark Angel could not control its own lust for sensation, it stripped away the control of its worshippers, enticing them towards every sick desire that had ever entered their minds. By possessing its cultists, the Dark Angel could vicariously indulge in the debauchery of lust, gluttony, wrath, and all the other sensations humans normally suppressed. Of course, this only made the thing more hungry.

Adam spied a number photographs around the perimeter of the supposedly disorganized living room, all facing the improvised altar, all of them of Holly or with her present. The girl was made to witness, even if only through the pictures. Her eyes further consecrated the heinous acts. Likely, Holly's sudden departure that night took the cult by surprise; they had intended for her to be here, to witness the rite. When she snuck out, she had forced a more symbolic witnessing.

The Dark Angel wants more than her body, it wants her innocence.

One photo, in particular, caught the hunter's attention. It rested in the center of the room, somewhat apart from the other photos, and had been strategically placed so that the victims and whoever had officiated the sacrifice would have an unobstructed view of the picture. Or rather, the picture would have an unobstructed view of them. In this, the only picture unstained and undamaged, the MacAllisters stood together, posed around a Christmas Tree. Each member was smiling. Holly looked to be only twelve or thirteen. Both parents had their hands on her. The father had his hand on his daughter's shoulder, forward a little too far, as though clutching her very possessively. He had leaned in, only the smallest fraction of a measurement, but noticeable to the right observer. The mother... her hand was on Holly's arm. It touched her daughter only barely, with the tips of the fingers. She stood only as close as was necessary for the picture. The mother had an area of separation between herself and the others.

Many other pictures offered a glimpse into his targets. Several images showed scenes of the small group from across time. Husband and wife in school, faces bright with hope and anticipation. A wedding, joyous and celebrant. The mother in higher schooling. A pregnancy, equally happy. Holly as a baby, with her father. The father in business, successful and proud. Mother and daughter, seemingly content. Smiles diminished as time went on, as did parental accomplishments. Holly's life continued but hers seemed the only one. Always there was that zone of separation between mother and daughter.

The hunter entered the master bedroom. The bed was disheveled, and unnecessarily so. A few drawers were open and overturned, with many standing untouched. The clothes were of good quality, with labels whose cost far exceeded their value. The remaining jewelry was also overly expensive, far in excess to what this family should own. Perfume and other feminine oddities all came from equally expensive sources. An image of his target began to form for the hunter.

He moved to the husband's possessions. The clothes were good but ordinary. He seemed to have only moderate tastes. A quick glance back at the photographs before Holly's birth showed vacations to exotic locations.

She desires more than she has, and her daughter cost her what she had.

The hunter nodded. Now he knew Elise MacAllister.

Although he had the information he needed and was ready to leave, Adam paused outside Holly's room. The door was slightly ajar. The hunter had no business within; there was no purpose in looking.

Adam gently pushed the door open until it bounced slightly against the wall. Her room was simple, even spartan. There was a single bed, well made, with bright blankets and pillows. A single desk rested with a chair in one corner, opposite the dresser and closet. The walls were undecorated except for a single board on which she had attached several photos, extracted magazine images, and drawn pictures. Adam looked closer and saw that the pictures were all of fantasy worlds from literature. She had organized them into some kind of narrative that made sense only to Holly.

Adam opened the closet to an amazing display of organization. Every piece of clothing was hung neatly. The shoes stood lined up as though for inspection. Each shelf had an obvious system of organization that Adam had no trouble discerning. He had heard of teenaged sloth and its tendency towards disorganized chaos, but he saw none of that here.

Her desk was clear of clutter. Only a small computer and lamp rested on it. In the center draw were letters of application to various universities, all out of state. Several acceptances with promises of academic scholarships. Each drawer was as overly-neat, as overly-organized as her closet. Nothing of great importance. He looked around the room, unsure of what he was looking for. His eyes fell again on the bed.

Adam sat down on it. The bed seemed to rest slightly higher than was necessary. He stood and turned, kneeling down to lift the blankets. Boxes rested beneath, from head to foot. He was about to turn away when a thought occurred. Adam pulled one of the boxes aside and spied a large wooden case behind. Clearly, she had used boxes on either side of the case to obscure it from casual view.

Adam pulled the case from under the bed. It was large and polished brightly without a single blemish or hint of dust. It had been so thick that it barely fit under the bed in the first place. A pair of simple brass latches secured the lid.

He released the latches. Resting within the case was a small folk harp. The wood and strings nearly shined with meticulous care. A small box with additional strings rested beside the harp, along with oil and other supplies. It was smaller than the harps Adam had seen before or those he remembered. It seemed specially fitted to a particular player with a uniquely carved shoulder leading down to the feet, stylized into Angelic wings.

Adam closed the lid and secured it. The hunter had learned all he needed and more besides. A glance outside Holly's window at the midday sun reminded him that he really did not have the time to waste on foolishness. He stood and scowled, leaving the MacAllister home and all the evil that had occurred there. The wooden case remained in Adam's secure grip.

Adam walked up the ally alongside his apartment complex. It was only a matter of hours before Holly would be sacrificed to whatever Dark Angel the cultists were worshipping. He knew the why, the how, and the when. He even had an approximate where, since Holly had told him that her father had obtained several military trucks. The only reason the cult would need those trucks was to get onto Fort Burleson. Unfortunately, that still left a huge area with no time to search it. He should NOT be wasting time with fool's errands, but should be doing everything in his power to locate the cult before they moved onto the military base.

Adam made a sound that as much a growl as it was a sigh. He hefted the case and entered the apartment complex.

Why the hell am I bothering with this?

It took only a few minutes to secure the case in his apartment and leave. As he appeared back onto the street, the hunter glared at the descending sun and cursed it for hurrying across the sky. If Elise MacAllister was so interested in her personal comfort, she would be hiding in one of the hotels of reasonable quality in the city. Adam did not have time to check every one. He needed some luck. Instead, something heavy struck him in the face.

17

For a while, the world spun around him. Adam fought to regain his senses as he was dragged somewhere. Blows rained down on him from all directions. He could not defend himself. There was no up or down. Pain came from everywhere. He could only wait and endure whatever his attackers decided to give him, hoping they did not want him dead.

"Stand him up." The command was given in a voice Adam thought he recognized. He fought to clear his sight, blinking and shaking his head, ignoring the throbbing, aching agony that flared throughout his body in response to every movement.

He was in an alley, somewhere near his apartment. Two large men, both Hispanic and covered with tattoos, held his arms tightly. Either one alone could have held him even were he not injured, together they insured that Adam went nowhere. Another three men, looking much like the first two, stood in front of him looking as intimidating as they could. Objectively, Adam thought they really did not need to bother, since the beating they had just given him had been plenty intimidating.

"Nice to see me again, *púto*?" the same voice asked.

"Huh?" Adam looked around but saw nothing. He then looked down. "Ah, Hell."

"That's right," Juan snarled. "It's payback time, bitch."

Adam shook his head. "What?"

"I said it's payback time!"

"I don't understand. You want a yak?"

"It's PAY. BACK. TIME!"

"Wow." He glanced at the thug on his right. "Is his accent this thick in Spanish, too?"

The thug shrugged.

Juan raged and waved his fists in the air. "You… You son of a… What… Why do you always gotta go racial? That's… that's just… that's just rude!"

"Sorry. If it's any comfort, I'm sure you'll be easier to understand once you hit puberty." Adam spat the accumulation of blood onto the ground. "Isn't your boss going to get pissed about this?"

Juan sneered. "Thanks to you, I'm in business for myself now, bitch."

"Well, look who's all grown up."

The pimp fumed some more before looking up at one of his thugs. "Well what hell are you grinning at? Do it!"

The beatings continued then. Adam had no sense of time as the men took turns beating him to the ground, picking him up, and then beating him back down again. They were clearly professionals, concentrating on his body, where damage could be maximized without risking unconsciousness or death. The fact that he was likely to be beaten to death by men who knew what they were doing came as little comfort, though.

"Enough," Juan commanded. He strutted over to where Adam lay on the ground, bleeding and gasping for breath. "Not so funny when you can't breathe, huh? Where are your jokes now, bitch?"

"Knock, knock," Adam said, through a mouth full of blood.

"That's cool," the pimp said. "I respect that." He looked around at his men. "This guy, he's a tough guy. He's gonna stay who he is 'til the end." Juan crouched down beside Adam. "Problem is, we ain't gonna kill you, bitch. Turns out, there's money on you. After you had your little fun this morning, I started askin' around 'bout you. Turns out, somebody wants your ass."

Seeing Adam look up, Juan smiled and nodded. "Yeah, it turns out when you keep pissin' people off, somebody is gonna get sick of it."

A police siren sounded nearby. Juan looked up in irritation. "One of you go pay them off."

"*Juan,*" a voice called from the end of the alley. "*Es El Llanero Solitario.*"

"*¿Qué?*" the pimp demanded.

"*Sí!*"

Juan cursed and barked orders to his men. He crouched low, hissing into Adam's ear. "Another time, fucker."

Adam lay there, hearing the retreat of his attackers. Another set of footsteps approached. As the light dimmed from his sight, he heard a familiar voice.

"Ah, damn. Please tell me I didn't just save you."

Adam awoke to pain. He was used to pain, so did not cry out. Instead, he opened his eyes and tried to sit up.

"Careful," a woman's voice warned. "You're busted up pretty good."

His vision cleared, and he slowly opened his eyes. Candace was kneeling beside him, holding his back. She was still not wearing that ridiculous ball cap, and her low cut t-shirt was stained with blood.

"How long was I out?"

"A few hours. I was starting to worry."

"Why," he grunted, "somebody hurt?"

The bartender smiled. "Yeah, somebody's hurt. Think you can lean back?" She gestured behind him.

Adam glanced back. He was on the floor of the Waystation. The bar was deserted except for the two of them. Candice wanted him to put his back to a booth and he obliged, ignoring the screams of protest coming from his back and ribs.

"Does it hurt?" she asked softly.

"Not much," he lied.

"Wait here." She stood and gathered the bloody remnants of an extensive first aid kit, which were scattered around the floor. Stashing the material behind the bar, Candice poured a glass of liquor and brought it back to Adam. "Slowly," she commanded. "It'll help with the pain you're lying about."

He grunted but obeyed. As he sipped at the welcome relief from reality, Adam noticed that his shirt was missing. His middles was now wrapped with bandages, likely holding his ribs in place. He also noticed that, with the necessity of tending his wounds at least temporarily relieved, Candice was very obviously trying not to notice the marks.

"I notice you noticing," he said softly.

"I wasn't going to ask."

Adam glanced down at his marks, but quickly had to look away. They were too strong a reminder of his past life. He was certain that, even in the culture of body art that abounded in this world, Candice had never seen anything quite like the dark, endless maze of First Language glyphs that decorated his flesh.

"That must have taken a long time."

"Yeah," he whispered.

"What does it mean?"

He hesitated. "They're names," Adam admitted for the first time to anyone. "Each time I was ordered to... act. I marked the name on myself so I would always remember."

Candice slowly reached out. Seeing that Adam was not going to stop her, she gently placed the tip of her fingers on his chest. The names, written in the First Language, that arcane text that had baffled scientists and wizards for centuries, were not listed in any straightforward way. Some were printed large, others small. Some went sideways, others long ways, and still others in a curve or spiral. The bartender ran her fingers along the strange pattern of Adam's history as it wound along his hard flesh.

"This is how you ignore pain," she whispered, looking up into his eyes.

He met her eyes but said nothing.

"Your heart hurts so much, so long... you can't feel pain anymore."

"Not just pain."

She leaned in, clearly wanting to help him. Their lips met then, very lightly. Candace made only the barest contact, holding her breath and closing her eyes against the endless suffering held behind Adam's eyes. Although unsure of what to do, something within Adam's unwanted soul responded, less to Candace's body or even her gesture, but rather to the feeling her lips conveyed. Compassion, empathy, catharsis. He reached a hand up, gently caressing her face, allowing for at least a moment of...

"I need my clothes," Adam said only slightly above a whisper. "I have to find Holly."

Candice nodded and stood. She reached down and helped him stand.

The flush of a toilet betrayed the fact they were not alone. Isandro emerged from the bathrooms adjusting his uniform. Noticing the emotions in the air and eyeing Adam and Candice's clasped hands, the good cop paused. "If I'm interrupting, I can go back and take a dump."

"Please tell me you're not the one who saved me," Adam sighed.

"You think I'm happy about it," he replied, moving towards the bar. "What did those punks want with you, anyway?"

"Not sure," the hunter replied, with Candice's help easing onto his favorite stool at the end of the bar. "They said something about a price on my head."

"I am so very surprised," Isandro said in a completely even voice, joining Adam at the next stool.

Candice went around behind the bar. "Drink?" she asked professionally.

The good cop held up a hand. "Still on duty." He looked over at Adam. "Does this price thing have anything to do with the MacAllister girl?"

"Probably. I've managed to kick up enough dirt that the bad guys will want me out of the way. They already tried buying me off."

"How much?"

"Anything I wanted, actually." Adam pushed back the glass Candice put in front of him. "Ice water," he requested. "Can't say I wasn't tempted," he said then, though to Isandro, or to Candice was unclear. The bartender smiled the barest hint of a smile and served the two men glasses of water, then rummaged under the bar for a large rag, shoveling into it handfuls of ice.

"Bullshit," Isandro snorted. "The only temptation you had was in not killing them all." He paused then, thinking and staring at Adam. "Does this have anything to do with what went on over in Markland?"

Adam shrugged. "They started it."

The good cop shook his head. "How is it that nobody can ever give an accurate description of you?" he mused, almost to himself. "You kick over every anthill in town, and still we're responding to 'adult male- average height, average build.' Hell, even the video witnesses shot of you comes out all blurry." He nodded at Adam's white leather coat. "You'd think people would just talk about that stupid coat."

Adam gratefully accepted the improvised ice pack Candice offered. "Most people don't notice the coat," he said, holding the ice to his head.

"How can you not notice an asshole in a leather jacket in the middle of summer?"

"Not sure how it works," Adam admitted. "It's just… people are encouraged not to notice it. Once you know it's there, then it's there. Until then…" he shrugged.

The good cop and bad Catholic stared for a minute at Adam before sharing a glance with Candice. "So," Isandro said, changing the subject from something his religion was not ready to consider. "Who's the bad guys?" he asked, raising the glass of water to his lips.

"A cult worshipping some, as-yet-unidentified Dark Angel."

"A what?" Isandro spit, along with a mouthful of water.

Adam sighed. "Angel's are real," he intoned, not for the first time, "God's real, Heaven's real. There really was a war, and a third of them really Fell."

Isandro sputtered a thousand questions at once.

"Does it matter what they're worshipping?" Candice interrupted, adjusting quickly to revelations normally reserved to hysterical mystics.

Adam shrugged again, still holding the comfortable relief of numbing cold against his skull. "It might. If I can get the girl before the ceremony, then no. If they manage to actually summon the damned thing then…"

"Wait," Isandro held up his hand. "Wait, wait, wait, wait." He took a deep breath. "Dark Angels? Cults? Magic leather coats? What kind of bullshit…?"

"Believe what you want." Adam glanced out the window at the fading light and sighed heavily. "It's starting to become moot, though. I needed to find where they were hiding the girl before the ceremony, but it's looking like that brilliant strategy won't work."

"Why not?" Candice asked.

"Not enough time. They'll be moving her to the site of the ceremony soon, so looking now would be a waste of what little time is left."

"Do you know where they'll be moving her?" Isandro asked, making an obvious physical effort to put aside cosmic implications in favor of letting the cop part of his brain assume control.

"Somewhere on Fort Burleson."

"Any chance of searching the base?" Candice asked, taking the melting ice pack from Adam and replacing it with a fresh one.

Isandro shook his head. "It's secured," he replied. "Nobody gets on that base without ID, which I doubt Mr. Lone-Gunman here has."

"Plus," Adam added. "That place is huge. The ceremony could be held anywhere." He sighed. "I have to track down exactly where on Fort Burleson the cult is meeting. If I don't, Holly is dead."

"What are your leads?" Isandro asked.

"The cult is filled with Agarés employees. There has to be some connection between Agarés and the base."

The good cop shook his head. "Agarés has buildings all over Fort Burleson. Warehouses, motor pools, labs. It would take weeks to search them all."

"Couldn't you talk to someone in Agarés?" Candice suggested.

Adam shook his head. "I already talked directly to Lilith Aubrey. Even she doesn't know anything about these people." He snorted. "Besides, she's probably too busy trying to chase down Hollman."

"Who?"

"Her assistant," Adam shrugged. "She's a member of the cult. I tried chasing her down myself, but she got away. Aubrey has people out looking, but right now that lead amounts to me sitting around, waiting for a call."

"Or you could ask her son," Candice suggested.

"What?" Adam asked.

"Who?" Isandro added.

"Her son. Well, that's what I'm guessing. He had the same last name."

Adam leaned in. "What are you talking about?"

"Mr. Date Rape from the other night?" Candice said. "The one you pulled off Holly? His last name was Hollman. It was on his ID, anyway."

Adam was silent. He leaned back, his mind racing. "So, the guy who tried to drug Holly has the same last name as one of the top members of the cult?"

Candice silently nodded her head.

Adam then looked over at Isandro.

"Congratulations," the good cop answered. "So stop sitting there feeling smart and go question the punk."

"Only problem," Adam mused. "I beat him half to death and left him lying in the street."

"Christ," Isandro prayed. "*That* was you too?"

"What?"

"A guy called 911 yesterday morning, saying he'd been jumped by some lunatic. By the time the paramedics got to him, he was almost dead. He's in the hospital."
Adam smiled at Isandro.
The good cop shook his head. "No. Hell no."

18

$\mathcal{R}$eese awoke to pain. The opiate fog that had kept him in bliss

had started to slip away, slowly bringing him back to consciousness. His swirling mind had trouble focusing on anything at first, but the pain gradually increased, beginning in his chest and lower back, then spreading down his legs. It grew until Reese could barely breathe, the memory of his injuries forcing him back into the awful reality of his hospital room.

Damn that lazy nurse! Momma is paying good money, and these simpletons can't even manage to keep the drugs coming. There's no reason for this. It's their damn job!

The young man did not bother opening his eyes as he reached for the call button, intent on giving that blue collar peasant a piece of his mind. Reese would definitely talk with his mother about the quality of care he had been receiving.

One of these hourly-wage rejects would pay for screwing up.

He kept jabbing at the call button, but the fool of a nurse did not respond. Reese opened his eyes and wished that his damaged face could form a properly dissatisfied snarl. With surprise, he noticed a doctor standing at the foot of his bed, reading the chart. "If you were standing there," the young man said through his wired jaw, "why didn't you say something?" The fact that his words, although eloquent, sounded whining and slurred through the damage to his face made Reese seethe even more.

"Reese Hollman," the doctor read. Holding the chart so high, Reese could not see the man's face. "Admitted early yesterday morning after suffering multiple contusions."

"Yeah, yeah," Reese sputtered in irritation. "I need more painkillers."

"Severe trauma." the doctor continued to read, ignoring his patient. "Broken ribs, severe damage to right hand, mild concussion, cracked jaw, and… ouch, testicular damage. Multiple surgeries. Prognosis: stable." The doctor finally lowered the chart, causing Reese's heart to freeze in the young man's chest. "Let's see what we can do about that."

It was *him*. Reese began frantically mashing the call button, desperate to summon help. He looked past the monster's shoulder towards the nurse's station, but saw nothing. There was no one. He was alone with the man who had beaten him nearly to death.

The monster put Reese's chart back in place and closed the privacy curtain. "Don't bother," he advised in a low voice. "I disabled the call button before I turned off your meds." With any view from the hall obscured, he pulled up a stool and sat down, looking at Reese with dead eyes. "It's good you remember me," he said. "That makes things simpler. You also remember that I'm the one who did this to you." He leaned in, very close. "We're going to have a conversation, Reese Hollman," he said, his voice having no emotion, no hint of any humanity.

Reese whimpered. He was trying to scream, but the damage to his face was too extensive.

"You should try to stay calm. With your jaw wired that way, if you get worked up, you could choke on your own saliva." He drew a knife. "If that happens, I'll have to cut open your throat to keep you breathing."

The heart rate monitor began frantically beeping. The monster stood and, after a brief search, found the button to silence the alarm. He then turned back. "You have information I want, Reese Hollman. You will give me that information. I have already given you pain. I will continue to give you pain until you give me the information I want. There is no one who can stop me. There is no one who can save you. If you take too long to give me the information that I want, I will kill you… slowly."

The colostomy bag began to rapidly fill.

"Do you want to live, Reese Hollman?"

The boy nodded frantically.

"Say it."

"I want to live," he gasped through his wired jaw.

"I'm going to start asking questions. Some of the answers I already know, and only ask to test your honesty. If you lie, you get pain. Do you understand?"

Again, Reese nodded.

"Say it."

"If I lie, you'll hurt me."

"Your mother's name is Isabel Hollman?"

Reese's eyes widened at the mention of his mother. He did not speak, but could only stare, trembling in fear. The monster put his fist against Resse's mangled groin and pressed in, twisting. Reese would have screamed if he could, writhing in agony.

"Failure to answer is worse than lying." He relented in the punishment. "Speak."

"Yes," Reese gasped. "She's my mother."

"She works at Agarés?"

"Yes. She's Ms. Aubrey's personal assistant."

"She is part of a cult that has been worshipping a Dark Angel? This cult has been abducting people to sacrifice for the creature?"

Again, Reese's eyes went wide. When he failed to answer, the monster moved his fist towards the boy's groin. Before more pain could be inflicted, however, the boy squeaked, "Yes!"

"Is she the leader of the cult?"

"No. She was recruited by the *Ímā*. They promised to make her the Regional Vice President of Agarés."

"Why was Isabel Hollman recruited?"

"She has access to resources they need. And, and they needed to keep an eye on Aubrey."

"You were brought into the cult as well?"

He did not speak, but only nodded.

"Your task was to secure the girl?"

Again, a nod.

"Why her? Why that girl, specifically?"

"It had to be her. The Angel demanded a sacrifice from the *Ímā*, as a sign of devotion. If we corrupted and sacrificed that girl, the Angel promised us all wealth and power."

"But why did your Angel want that girl?"

Reese hesitated, wanting more than almost anything not to reveal the terrible truth only a handful knew, that his mother had only learned from her seduction of the father, and only shared with Reese during a drunken diatribe expressing her disgust with the entire family.

The monster leaned in, his eyes holding no soul, no humanity, only impossible purpose. "Speak," he commanded.

"The Angel didn't demand her," Reese almost choked. "The *Ímá* offered Holly. The Angel only wanted someone innocent, someone good and pure. It was the *Ímá*'s idea to give Holly."

A snarl crawled onto the monster's face. The icy Hell in his eyes was replaced with a burning damnation. He leaned in until the hatred in his breath singed the hairs on Reese's face. "Where are they keeping her?" the monster demanded.

"An Agarés warehouse!" Reese quailed.

This answer seemed to infuriate the monster. He gritted his teeth.

Desperate to appease his torturer, the boy offered more. "But it's too late! They've already gone to…" he clamped his lips shut.

"To Fort Burleson," the monster finished. He reached into the lab coat he wore, fishing out a map of the military base. Unfolding it, the monster held it in front of his victim. "Point. If you lie, if you're wrong, if you delay me. I will come back. I will take you away from here." He stared holes into Reese's soul. "You will take days to die."

With a bandaged, trembling hand, the same hand the monster had destroyed, Reese pointed, betraying his mother and fellow devotees.

The monster looked at the spot on the map that his target had pointed towards, far from any building, in the wilderness of the training areas. There were many hills in that area, and even a small cave system marked on the map. The monster nodded with approval. He turned back to Reese.

"I'm going to let you live," he said. "If you haven't lied to me, I won't come back. Once the doctors finish repairing you, leave this area."

"It doesn't matter," the young man replied. "There are over a hundred of us. Go there. Try to stop us. We have cops, soldiers, guns. What do you have? A knife? They're going to finish the ritual and the Angel is going to give the *Ímá* great power."

The monster stepped away, making to leave.

"Your little bitch is going to die tonight! The Angel will rape her soul!"

The monster stopped.

He looked back at Reese.

He calmly walked over to the bed. The monster looked down for a moment, and then securely strapped down Reese's arms. He then turned to the IV that was supposed to be feeding drugs into the young man and pulled the line free of the machine. Looking into Reese's eyes, he held the tube to his mouth and breathed deeply into the plastic line before plugging it back into the machine.

"What are you doing?" Reese demanded frantically.

The monster turned the machine back on. The medication began working its way back through the tube, pushing the air forward, towards Reese's arm. The monster leaned in, grabbing his victim's wrist and pinning it to the bed. Even as the lethal bubble reached Reese's arm and entered, the monster's gaze never blinked, never wavered.

Isandro was waiting at the other end of the hall with the three nurses on duty, Adam's white leather coat rolled into a tight ball and held under his arm. The dashing cop had all of the ladies laughing at his exaggerated tales of law enforcement, blissfully unaware of the intruder who had just murdered one of their patients. Each of the women, from the teenaged-appearing youngest to the middle-aged oldest, seemed to vie with one another in their attempts to gain Isandro's attention. To his credit, the loving cop showered each with devotion, laughing at every attempt at humor, complementing every mention of minor achievement, and shamelessly admiring every physical attribute. Had he wanted to, the man-whore could probably have convinced any one, or perhaps all, of those nurses to join him for an evening interlude.

Adam caught his accomplice's attention and jerked his head towards the exit. The good cop nodded slightly and made apologies, insisting that his duties, harsh as they were, demanded that he leave. With promises to return another time, Isandro walked away, blessing each of the women with one last shining smile.

"You really are a slut, aren't you?" Adam asked once Isandro caught up, pulling off the stolen lab coat and absently tossing it onto an empty wheelchair. He then accepted back his white leather coat from the good cop, throwing the rough garment over his broad shoulders.

Isandro shrugged. "I also have two phone numbers and something to do this weekend, how about you?"

Adam stopped in the hallway and leaned against a wall. He shook his head.

"What is it?" the good cop asked. "He didn't give up the info?"

"Oh, he gave it up. It's just a lot worse than I thought."

"Well?"

Again, Adam shook his head. "There's too many."

"You're kidding, right?" Isandro snorted. "You? Worried about the odds? You've spent the last two days running around this town kicking ass and only *now* you're worried about the odds?"

Adam looked up into the other man's eyes. "It's different this time," he admitted. "It's not just my ass...."

Isandro nodded. "It's easy when it's just us." He moved to the opposite side of the hall and, leaning against it, crossed his arms over his chest. "Things get a lot more complicated when you have to start risking someone else."

"This whole thing has been about getting that girl out of trouble. If it was just me getting shot at or catching a beating, so be it. But now, if I fail..."

"She dies," Isandro finished. "How bad are the odds?"

"He said they've got a hundred. Cops and soldiers included. Armed and ready. They know I'm out here, looking for the girl."

"So... the odds suck."

Adam snorted.

"What's the play?"

Adam shook his head. "I don't know. If I go in... I die. If I die, she dies. If I don't go in... I live, she dies. They have the cops, they have the military. What do I have?"

The world then paused. Adam recognized the effect almost immediately. Isandro and the other humans in the hallway froze in place, held by Celestial power. The subtle sounds in the hospital all silenced. Even the air itself, circulated by the building's machines, paused. It was as though Adam were the only living figure in a photograph.

Then, the thunk of a soda falling from a vending machine disturbed the peaceful stillness. Simkiel stood at the far end of the hallway, retrieving the can he had just purchased.

Adam snarled in fury and lunged, hurling himself at the Angel. Grabbing him by the front of his designer suit, the hunter slammed his enemy into the wall. "WHY!?!" Adam demanded. "What do you bastards want from me!?! Don't tell me this is all a coincidence, I KNOW BETTER!!! You put me in this situation just to kill me off!?! A hopeless battle to save an innocent!?! To watch another girl die!?! Why involve her!?! If it's me you want, JUST KILL ME!!!"

Simkiel smiled and held up the soda. "Drink?" he asked calmly.

The hunter smacked the can away. "You're going to help her, damn you!" Adam snarled, holding a finger in the Angel's face. "Enough of this 'moving in mysterious ways' bullshit! Enough free will excuses! You will get off your holy ass and *do something!*"

The Angel just looked down at the raging hunter and sighed. "That's not how we work, and you know it. Humans hurt humans; humans save humans. It's not for the Chorus to interfere. Free Will must…"

"ENOUGH!!!" Adam roared, slamming the Angel into the wall with such force the plaster cracked. "Enough of your hypocrisy! Enough of your half-truths! Enough of your stalling! They're suffering *now*! They need help *now*! And all you bastards do is sigh and say, 'Free Will must determine their fate?' NO MORE!!!"

The hunter threw Simkiel to the floor. Standing over the Angel, Adam Kadmon pointed a finger. "Know this," he thundered. "Even if you bastards refuse to help them, *I* won't! There has to be at least one Angel on Earth who still believes in protecting humanity!"

Without another word, Adam stepped over his one-time brother and walked away, almost heedless of time resuming its normal course. Isandro blinked at Adam's apparent disappearance, but recovered quickly and moved to join the other man in his course. Unseen by either, still lying where Adam had thrown him, Simkiel's face betrayed the slightest smile.

"So, what's the plan?" Isandro asked as they left the hospital. "I only ask because, last I checked, we were still pretty screwed."

Adam paused and looked up. The sky had gone dark. The pregnant moon was beginning her climb. They had only a few short hours before the ritual would begin, and Holly would be… Isandro was correct that, despite Adam's declaration that he would not abandon the girl, their chances of success had not improved. None of that mattered, however; he would *not* fail.

Adam looked to his friend. "Can you create some kind of false alarm big enough that all the cops will be called in?"

"I don't know," Isandro replied. "Maybe. What're you thinking?"

"The biggest advantage the bad guys have is numbers and guns. I want to wear that down."

The good cop nodded. "If I call in an anonymous bomb threat to a major building like city hall, that'll kick up enough trouble that they might call everybody in."

Adam thought for a moment. "I think I can do one better. Let's have one called in from Agarés."

"How are you going to manage that?"

He grinned and pulled a business card form the side pocket of his white leather coat. "I have an in. Besides, I'll need Aubrey to get me a few things anyway."

"Us," Isandro replied. "You suck as a white hat. I'm going too."

Adam shook his head. "It'll be hard enough for me to pull this off. I need you to keep the cops busy when I go in. Besides, if I die, somebody who knows what those bastards did needs to stay alive."

"It's not right," the good cop grumbled. "You shouldn't have to face this alone."

"I'm used to it." Adam paused. "I appreciate it though."

"Oh, God, please stop. We're starting to bond. Let's just get this done."

19

        *A*dam had his not-quite-friend drop him off at his apartment. He walked into his bedroom and took off his white leather coat. There was something he needed if he was going to have any success that night. It was dark in the bedroom, and Adam thought that was proper, since he was going to a very dark place.

Since coming to Disanté, he had tried very hard to forget his old life. His old memories, both good and bad, were a source of constant pain to Adam. The good ones only served as a reminder of all that he had lost and could never have again. The bad ones, most powerful of all, plagued him with all the things he had done and wanted desperately to escape. Adam had dedicated nearly every waking moment over the past two months to trying to suppress what he had been, because what he had been was a monster. Now, to save a girl's life, he must not just release that monster, but embrace it fully.

He reached under the bed and retrieved a pair of leg harnesses. They appeared to be leather. The material was pliable like leather and even had the same flesh coloring. The harnesses molded perfectly to his powerful thighs as Adam buckled on the sheaths. There was writing of the First Language branded onto each of them, much as something would be burnt onto leather.

The sheathes were nearly indestructible. In all the battles he had ever fought, nothing had ever harmed them. Fire had not burned them. Blades had not cut them. He had sometimes wished that Adam's flesh were made of the same mystical material. Had it been so, perhaps he would not have suffered so many injuries nor carried so many scars on the body or in the heart.

With the sheathes in place on his legs, Adam turned and retrieved from under the bed a large wooden case. Pushing aside the similar case holding Holly's harp, he placed his own on top of the blankets that Holly had gotten for him and stared. His old life rested within. He could sense them, calling to him, eager for use. He heard them singing to him, whispering as sweetly as any lover. They knew him better than any other who had lived or ever would. And they should, they had been at his side for his entire life.

They love me, they smoothed my life's rough course.

He took a deep breath and opened the case, and the small scrap of a soul that had formed within Adam Kadmon retreated from the blades. It could not bear the presence of such destruction. The moment the hunter put his hands on his oldest friends, his truest companions, he felt better than he had in months, for he felt nothing at all. They were perfect, and they completed him. The aching hole in his breast filled as he picked them up. The hilt of each blade fit perfectly in his hand. The weapons were fitted exactly for him, specific tools for a specific hand. Rather than the common swords of any mundane warrior, these one-sided blades projected at a perpendicular from the base of the hilt so that they could rest gently against his arms. Standing in the center of that dark room, the hunter felt like himself, or at least, a welcome shadow of his true self.

The metal of the blades was flawless. The hunter held them up and gazed at his tools in near-reverence. More of the First Language adorned each of them, warning his victims of their immanent destruction. A slight flick of the wrist, and the weapons rolled in the hunter's hands, the blades spinning and now reaching out in front of his outstretched arms. The blades were deadly extensions of his arms, with their sharpened edges facing outwards. The passage of these blades cut everything, matter, air, even thought itself.

An absolute calm descended over the hunter as he refamiliarized himself with his blades. They danced together, as they had in his previous life. They sang together as all that was good and kind, and fearful and uncertain within Adam Kadmon fled back to the darkened corner of the hunter's being where they could not interfere with what must be. There was no longer doubt. There was no longer compassion or regret. There was only the hunter.

The enemies that would soon face him would be nothing more than temporary obstacles. He felt no pity or remorse for them; he *could* feel no pity or remorse. Any that stood against him would fall. It was their decision and thus, their responsibility. The aching despair that had so pulled at Adam Kadmon for these past months was gone.

There was nothing as the hunter stood in his place. Every emotion retreated. He was a soulless creature, a destroyer.

Letting the blades slide downwards once again, the hunter sheathed them. He retrieved Adam Kadmon's white leather coat and put it on, ensuring that the garment would not interfere with the quick deployment of his weapons. Satisfied that he was ready, the monster wearing Adam's face went outside.

Something hard came swinging towards that face. The hunter caught it and struck at the attacker with fists and feet.

"Nice reflexes *púto!*" Juan snarled. The short pimp, again surrounded by his much larger men, had gathered around the apartment's front door for another ambush. The fact that the surprise attack had not been as immediately successful as the first did not seem to bother them. "That's not gonna save you though! Nobody around to stop us!"

The hunter pulled the edges of his coat back, exposing the hilts of his blades.

"Hey, nice knives!" Juan said mockingly. "I think I'll use them to cut your balls off!" he pushed at the shoulder of one of his men. "Get this fool!"

Less than a minute later, only Juan remained alive. The bloody remains of his men were scattered around the front of the apartment complex. The small pimp, the bloody stump of his right arm clutched to his chest, scrambled on the ground away from the advancing monster. "*Eres el Diablo!*" he sobbed.

The hunter paused a moment to consider. "*No; soy peor que el Diablo.*" He then raised his blades and slashed across Juan's face, bringing a scream of pain and terror, but leaving the criminal alive. He was, after all, a good source of information and could possibly remain one now that this lesson in obedience had been administered. As the hunter departed, Juan held a trembling hand to the two diagonal slashes across his face and realized he had soiled himself.

The hunter went to a nearby row of tall, narrow sheds. Most of the apartment tenants used these for long-term storage. Adam Kadmon had stored only one thing within his assigned space. Only days after his arrival in Disante, he had encountered the police sergeant Isandro. The good cop had been under attack by a criminal with knowledge of the mystical and supernatural. Adam had killed that man, saving the good cop's life. The resulting victory had gained Adam two prizes. The first was the white leather coat. The second he stored within the shed.

The hunter raised the heavy metal door and stepped inside, turning on the small overhead light. A tarp covered the Beast, as it had since Adam first stored it here. "I need you," the hunter said. "I understand a promise was made, but the situation has changed." He stepped closer. "Adam Kadmon freed you from the sorcerer who trapped you in this form. There was no demand of repayment. Only a promise that, should he find the means to restore you, he would do so. You would never be used as a slave as Simon had done, so I will not force you. I will only explain the situation and ask." He pulled the tarp aside.

Underneath was what appeared to be a motorcycle. The handlebars rose up, out, and down, so that the rider's arms rode wide as he controlled the vehicle. The front suspension frames formed a pair of legs like those of a predatory cat, extending the front wheel away from the main body. The seat was lower than the large gas tank, black leather that sharply contrasted the highly chromed detailing. The twin exhaust and mufflers beneath the raised passenger seat bore a license plate that read, "Beast." It was a cruiser built for comfort, power, and intimidation.

"A girl has been taken," the hunter said to the Beast. "She is little more than a child. Her own mother intends to sacrifice her to a Dark Angel. You know what the creature will do to the girl before it kills her. They have a hundred followers, ready to die for their leader, and I am alone. The Choir will not intercede.

The hunter stood in front of the machine. "I know your suffering. I know what it is to be trapped in a form not your own. To suffer in a life you did not ask for. I would not disturb you from your misery except to ask that you help me save this innocent. Will you come with me? Will you fight with me?"

A pair of headlights, vertical slits that burned with amber fire, ignited, even as the engine roared to life.

The hunter mounted the Beast. "To battle then."

The Beast roared its agreement as they rode into the night.

Aubrey stood in the front parking lot of Agarés with two of her bodyguards. Kadmon had called twenty minutes ago with specific requests. In the interests of their continued understanding, Aubrey had agreed. She now waited with growing impatience. "How long?" she demanded of one of the fools who were supposed to protect her.

The guard checked his watch. "Five minutes."

The executive seethed. She did not like to be kept waiting. He had given a meeting time for five minutes ago. Granted, Kadmon did not seem like the punctual type, but Aubrey was meticulous about her schedule. With the added pressure of the upcoming time limit for her arrangement with the Dark Angel, the woman was becoming increasingly agitated.

She was about to demand yet another update of the time when a motorcycle roared into the parking lot bearing Kadmon. Aubrey sneered at the ostentatious arrival.

Just like a man to need something so loud and...

Kadmon pulled to a stop in front of them and dismounted. Aubrey cleared her throat. "Well," she said contemptuously, "it's about time."

He turned to face her, ignoring the guards. "You have it?" he asked with a deep voice that reached out to her, pulling at her body in places deep and low.

Aubrey cleared her throat and focused her mind. "Before we get to that, I think we need to get a few things straight Mr. Kadmon."

Kadmon walked forward with that same, blank expression. One of the guards moved to intercept him but was sent, screaming, to the ground with a broken arm and crushed nose. The second guard reached for his gun. "No!" Aubrey tried to warn him.

It was too late. The second guard had his weapon taken away and turned against him. A single shot sent the dead man falling to the ground. Throughout the engagement, Kadmon had never paused in his advance towards Aubrey.

He did not pause even when he reached her, instead pushing her back against her car with the unstoppable mass of his emotionless stride. Aubrey was forced off-step, stumbling for only an instant before Kadmon grabbed her, holding her up with as little effort as one would hold a tiny doll. He caught the back of her neck with one hand and put the other around Aubrey's throat. Caught off guard, stunned by his unrelenting force and the soulless voids that had replaced his eyes, she could do nothing.

"Aubrey," he said in a voice so deep it seemed to arise from the earth. His hand slid from her throat down the front of her blouse. "You will learn." Her breath came in jagged gasps as his powerful hand pushed in and down, along her chest and stomach until it reached the front of her pants. "I always get want I want," he continued in that same deep, cold voice, that voice that seemed filled with all of Lilith's deepest fears and desires. He continued to stare with dead eyes into her frantic heart. She realized that, to this man, she was nothing more than an object, a thing to be used. "You will give me what I want, before I take it." Kadmon then held up the small packet of paperwork he had retrieved from her front pocket.

He then let Lilith go, causing her to fall and land on her backside. Without another word, nor even a backwards glance, Kadmon returned to his motorcycle and roared away. Lilith continued to stare in shock after him, desperately trying to gather her wits and steady her trembling body.

20

There was a needle in Holly's neck.

Is that Dad? I don't understand.

They were forcing her into a van. They were putting a bag over her head.

Why can't I move? Am I tied down? I want to go home. I'm scared. I don't understand. Why is this happening? What did I do? The drinks burn so much I can barely taste the apple. Is there something in these? I feel so strange. Is this my fault? Adam is so mad. How do I know his name? He's so angry, but he's angry at everything, especially himself. Is he angry at me, too? I was only trying to do something nice. He's doing so much. Oh God! Look at how hurt he is. This is my fault! It's all my fault! Why is Dad here!?! What's he doing? Why is this happening!?! I'm sorry! I just want to go home! Why can't I go home!?!

Music filled Holly's mind then. She could not remember the melody at first, nor did she understand from where it came. Still, something in that sense memory, that emotional fragment called out through the years, through the confusion, through the terror, and wrapped its gentle arms around her heart. It was the gentle lullaby her uncle had taught her, years ago while Holly was first learning to play the harp. They would play it together, she on the harp and he on the guitar.

Holly thought of the notes, of forming the chords with her fingers. She thought of her uncle singing along. Her terror receded. The nightmarish real world with its monsters and its evils kept crashing against the warm love of her uncle and the harp lessons, the last gift he gave her before... The dark storm of her captivity could make no purchase against the calm mechanics and serene expression of her harp.

After some endless time, an eternal, exhausting sleep, Holly opened her eyes. She could not focus completely, but she could begin to make out her surroundings. She was in the back of a truck, one of those army trucks she saw driving around Fort Burleson. It was not moving, but the engine was running. She started to move, fighting against what felt like lead in her veins and lifting herself up from the truck's bed. She was stiff, as though she had been lying on the floor for hours. She still had the broken chains from the warehouse on her ankles and wrists, but they were not connected to anything. She could start to move, but she had to do so carefully, to keep the chains from making noise.

Holly crawled to the edge of the truck and peeked through the edge of the tarp covering the back. They were at East Gate, one of the side entrances onto Fort Burleson. She recognized the fences, floodlights, and signs. A few soldiers stood nearby, talking with Holly's dad.

"You're good to go, sir," one of the soldiers was saying.

"Good," Dad was saying. "We've had enough screw-ups already. Have any of the others been through yet?"

"Yes sir, most of them are already through."

"And the *Ímã*?"

"Her car passed through about an hour ago, sir."

Holly's dad nodded. "Alright, then let's not keep her waiting." He gestured to two other men standing nearby. "You two, she should be out for another few hours, but ride in back, just in case."

Shit!

With no more time to spare, Holly lunged towards the back, grabbing the truck's gate and vaulting over. The large drop from the tall truck surprised her, but still she was able to roll with the impact on the city street. Holly then scrambled to her feet and sprinted as fast as her stiff legs could carry her.

"What the fuck!?!"

There was a snap and hiss, then searing pain lanced into Holly's back. All her muscles stiffened and contorted, sending waves of agony through her. She did not remember falling to the ground, only lying there as the pain eventually faded into a deep ache. Her heart rammed against her chest and she could not stop her body from jerking in random, painful ways.

Her dad stepped into view. He was holding something that looked like a gun in his hand, trailing two thin wires into her back. He knelt next to his daughter and gently brushed a few stray hairs from her sweat-drenched face. "You always were tougher than people thought," he said fondly, brushing a light finger along her lips. "If only," his eyes drifted down, along his daughter's writhing body. "Oh, well." He stood and pointed the gun-thing at Holly, pulling the trigger and the world went dark again.

Holly awoke to pain. The world spun was spinning. Her mouth was dry, and her throat was burning. Her entire body ached; there was nothing that did not scream in protest when she tried to move.

"She's awake," someone to the right said. "Get the *Ímā*."

Holly risked opening her eyes again and, happily, noticed that her vision had straightened itself out. She looked around. She was in a cave. All around were brown walls, like being inside a log of shit, marked with the same weird writing from that warehouse. The only reason she could see anything was all the candles these cultist assholes had put everywhere.

Like it needed to be any hotter.

The weirdoes had undone the metal manacles on her wrists and ankles, and left her lying in some corner of a small, dead-end tunnel. They had also taken all her clothes off.

"Son of a bitch!" she seethed aloud.

Holly looked around for something to cover herself with but could see nothing. The small room they had put her in was empty. Empty except for a naked, really pissed off woman. The only thing she could think to do was back up against the wall, pull her short legs up, and wrap her arms around them. To make matters worse, she noticed, the sick freaks had also painted some more of their voodoo letters all over her skin... *all* over. Holly had tried for years to get her parents to let her get a tattoo, but this was ridiculous.

"Enjoying the view, perv?" she sneered at her guard, noticing his gaze.

The robed letch smiled and kept looking. He was pretty young. He even had acne. Holly was not sure, but thought she recognized him. Having graduated from high school last spring, there were a lot of faces that she knew would fade from memory. This guy's face was not all that remarkable to begin with, so it would not be that great a leap to think that she had never bothered to learn it in the first place. His boney frame and bad smell certainly did not help in jogging Holly's memory, nor in endearing him to her. Not to mention the gun strapped to his hip.

It's bad enough that I get kidnapped. But to get taken by these rejects!

Holly desperately considered any possibilities. She knew Adam was looking for her. He had found where they were holding her at least once already; it could only be a matter of time before he found her again. If she sat tight and stayed alive, she had a chance. The girl quickly dismissed that thought, though. It would be foolish to pin all her hopes on that. Holly had escaped from these dorks before, she could do it again.

Once more noticing how the guard's eyes were staying on certain parts of her body, Holly got an idea. It turned her already weak stomach, but given her situation, she had few options. "Do you think it was such a good idea that they left me alone with you?" As she spoke, Holly let her arms loosen from around her legs, falling around her ankles.

"I'm pretty sure I can handle you."

She dropped her eyes to the ground and began to lightly run her fingertips up her legs. "That's kind of my point," she said softly. "I'm surprised they trust you."

"I do what I'm told." His eyes remained fixed on the motion of her hand.

Holly kept her knees together, but let her hand slide between her legs, slowly moving towards her lap. She took a deep breath. "Always?"

The guard's breathing, unlike Holly's, was not deep, but shallow and uneven. "Stop that," he tried to growl. It came out as more of a squeak, though.

The girl pulled a hand up, cupping a small breast. "Yes, sir."

He took an involuntary step towards her, his hand twitching in sympathetic sensation.

Holly raised her eyes to his and moved her other hand into her lap. Moving her knees apart, just enough to offer a hint, she took another deep breath. "What else do you want me to do?"

"Alright," a new voice said," stop that."

Holly's seducee straightened and blushed, looking ashamed of himself. The girl flinched back into her defensive ball at the newcomer's voice.

That voice…

"Mom?"

Elise MacAllister stepped into the light of her daughter's cell. Holly stared in shock as her mother looked down at her with a kind smile. "Hello, honey," Elise said in the same soft voice she had used to welcome Holly home from school for as long as she could remember. It was the same voice full of acceptance but missing… something. "I imagine you have a few questions." Elise turned to the guard, brushing back her long dark hair, the perfect match to Holly's, though now streaked with grey. "Timothy, would you excuse us? I'd like to have a word with my daughter."

Timothy bowed deeply. "Of course, *Ímā*," he replied with profound respect, and left them alone.

Elise turned back to Holly and folded her hands in front of her expanding waist, the same as she had done in front of her apron when talking to her daughter in the kitchen. "I guess this is all pretty confusing, huh?"

Holly could only nod mutely.

"I'm sorry we had to lie to you, honey," Elise said. She rubbed at her wrinkled eyes. "Your dad and I are trying to do something here and… well, it's really complicated."

"Complicated? You faked your deaths. You had me kidnapped. And… hello, naked."

"Yeah, about that," Elise shrugged slightly. "I'm afraid your dad and I need… well we sort of need a favor from you."

"What? What favor?"

"Well, you see, when people start to get older and they realize that their lives aren't going to turn out the way that they had planned, they start wondering if there isn't a way to change those lives. Your dad and I found a way. With your help, we'll be able to help a lot of people in this city to make good changes in their lives. They'll be smarter, stronger, more attractive, even younger. They'll be able to use these gifts to have a positive effect on the community, maybe even the whole world."

"Uh huh. And where do I come in?"

Elise smiled. "Well, honey. Believe it or not, you're the most important part. I know you and your dad have been arguing for a while now about what you were going to do with your life, where you were going to go. But you don't have to worry about any of that from now on. We've chosen a path *for* you. I always knew you were special honey, I just didn't know what was special about you. Now I do.

"You see, we need you to be a part of a very special ritual. Once this ritual is complete, all the people I've been trying to help will get everything they've ever wanted. Why, even I will get great gifts. I'll be healed." She held a hand over her abdomen and smiled brightly at her daughter. "You can finally make the hurt that you gave mommy go away; don't you want that?"

Tears formed in Holly's eyes at the mention of an old injury, rarely mentioned, but always present. "Mom…"

Elise held up a hand. "Don't worry, honey," she interrupted. "It's ok. Yes, it was your fault, but that's over now. You can finally make it all better." She turned back towards the tunnel. "Timothy, Heberto? Would you two come back in please?"

Holly looked past towards the approaching guards. "Mom, I don't understand," she said in fear.

The two men, one a boy and the other an older man, entered and faced their leader. "Thank you," Elise said upon their entrance. "It's just about time," she told them. "Would you two take Holly to the altar and have the others make sure she's ready?"

"Yes ma'am," the older one said, bowing.

"And make sure she's not hurt," Elise reminded them with a stern wag of her finger. "The Angel demands that she be as pure as possible."

The two guards bowed again and turned to Holly.

"What are you doing?" the girl yelled. "Mom! What is this!?! ARE YOU INSANE!?!"

They pulled her up, ignoring the blows Holly tried to land on them. The guards grabbed her firmly, securing her hands without causing any unnecessary damage, and started dragging her into the tunnels. While this went on, Elise looked on with an unflinching smile.

"Mom!" Holly desperately called out. "Please, you can't do this! MOOOOMMMM!!!!"

21

 Edward MacAllister reached the entrance to the caves, huffing with the exertion. He was glad that the night of the ceremony had finally arrived, it would be nice to be free of his aging body. The two guards he had placed at the cave's mouth stood there still, but looked very anxious, and welcomed the arrival of their leader's husband with obvious relief.

"Sir," the younger, Sam, sighed. "Thank God."

Edward made a sharp motion with his hand. "You know that word is forbidden," he reproached. "On this night especially. The Angel will not tolerate his devotees uttering it."

Sam nodded. "I'm sorry, sir," he replied. "It's just…"

Tyler put a comforting hand on his brother's shoulder. "Things are getting a little weird out here," he confessed.

"What do you mean weird?" Edward asked.

Tyler shrugged. "It's hard to explain. Ever since all the others left, we've been getting… I don't know…"

"Scared," Sam finished.

"Are you sure you're not just nervous?" Edward asked. "Tonight's a big night. It's understandable to be a little worked up about it. Especially after we had to send all our best men out to deal with that bomb at Agarés."

Sam shook his head and looked out, into the surrounding darkness. Thick clouds had plunged the hills all around them into deep darkness, so that nothing could be seen beyond the small circle of light provided by the lantern at the cave's entrance. "It's just so… still," the boy whispered.

Tyler nodded. "Shouldn't there be some animals or something out here?" he asked.

Edward sighed, growing a little impatient. "Don't forget this is an Army base," he reminded them. "With all the running around the soldiers do, I doubt that there're all that many animals out here. I mean, would *you* want to live out here with tanks driving around all the time?"

"I guess not," Tyler agreed.

"And as far as the 'stillness,' don't forget that this is a very holy night. There are great powers at work. The *Ímá* has said that we will all see something very special tonight."

The boys both nodded.

Edward patted both of them on the backs. "Now, with our police and soldiers gone, I'm really going to need you boys to step up, alright? And don't forget, we have guards out there patrolling. If anything happens, or anyone tries to sneak up on you, they'll let you know."

"That's why we called you, sir," Tyler said. "We've been trying to call the guards for fifteen minutes, and nobody's responding."

Edward thought about it. "That's odd." He looked around at the tall hills and shrugged. "Well, with all this terrain blocking the radios, it probably just means they can't hear you calling. Once the sentries realize they've lost contact, they'll come back. Give it a few more minutes, and if you still haven't heard anything, let me know and we'll get a few people together and go looking for them."

The two boys nodded at the older man's reasoning. Edward again patted them on the backs and turned to leave. "Give me a call if anything happens," he said in parting.

Returning to the cave's main chamber, the older man shook his head. Isabel Hollman joined him on the outskirts of the circle of the faithful as the preparations for the ceremony continued. "Everything alright outside?" she asked.

He nodded. "They're just rattled," he replied.

"I think we all are," she said. They calmly watched as Holly, finally having ended her pathetic pleas to her indifferent parents, was bound to the altar in the center of the chamber. "Having so many of our strongest get called away at so important a time is not a good omen," Hollman continued.

Edward continued to watch a small group of the faithful use chains to secure his daughter. "Better that the disruption is happening in town and not nearby," he reasoned. "It likely means the Fallen One is there and not here. Besides, our brothers and sisters will still reap the benefits from tonight, even if they're not here."

"So your wife says."

He glanced at Hollman. "You have doubts?"

She shrugged, running a hand along the low neckline of her blouse. Hollman, unlike most of the older women among the faithful, had yet to lose most of her physical beauty and enjoyed flaunting that fact by wearing revealing clothes to every gathering. While their female members had, on occasion, voiced some objection to this, the male members had no particular problems.

"Even on this night you have to dress so provocatively?" Edward demanded wearily.

Hollman raised an eyebrow and smiled without bothering to look his way. "I don't recall you objecting to what I wore last Thursday," she reminded him.

"Can you even imagine what she would do to us if she found out?" he demanded in a low voice.

"What makes you think she cares? You wife has been obsessed with the Angel for months." Hollman nodded towards where Elise had taken up position to stand beside the altar, looking down at her daughter. "I'm a little surprised she didn't volunteer to lie on that slab herself. After all, the chance to fuck an Angel must be very tempting."

"Not everyone is obsessed with sex," Edward growled.

Hollman laughed, very softly. "No, just you. Others of us understand that it's useful towards an end." She turned to face him. "But just imagine, after tonight, your wife will be fertile again, young and beautiful like your daughter. Maybe you can bring yourself to start sleeping with her again; you won't have to screw around, asking other women to dress and act like little Holly. Maybe someday she'll even lighten up enough to try some of the sick shit I was willing to do." With that, she turned and stepped down, into the lower section of the central chamber, where the rest of the faithful were gathering into a ring.

Before Edward could also join in the ceremony, the radio on his belt squawked. "What now," he barked into it.

"SIR!!! HE'S HERE!!! HE'S… AIIIIIEEEEEE!!!!" The filled with static.

Edward's heart froze in his chest. He stared at the radio, unsure of what to do. Every eye in the cave was turned towards him, having heard the outburst. And then, the radio came alive one last time.

"That's right," a voice, dark and evil, growled. "I'm here. I found you."

Chained to the altar, Holly laughed in gleeful anticipation. "You're all *fucked* now!"

Edward MacAllister emerged from the cave with most of the remaining cultists. A dozen men and women stood with him, all armed with a variety of weapons. Inside, Elise and Isabel led four other women in continuing the ritual around Holly, under the guard of four men.

A hasty plan had been put together, under Holly's constant mockery. Edward MacAllister would lead most of the cultists outside, delaying the Fallen One long enough for the *Ímā* to complete the ritual. So long as Edward and the others could delay the monster long enough, the Angel would appear and defeat their enemy. Having the most dangerous part of the plan, Edward had objected, but been overruled by the *Ímā*. He had looked to Isabel for support, but seen only a cold indifference.

"How's it feel to be the one under the knife, *Dad?*" Holly had mocked.

Edward MacAllister had not replied, but just accepted the rifle Isabel offered and began climbing the stone steps out of the chamber.

"Hey, Dad?" Holly had called out.

Edward had glanced back.

"He's going to cut your fucking heart out!"

They found the remains of Tyler and Sam scattered around the entrance of the cave. No piece larger than a hand remained intact. Gore was everywhere. Their blood seemed to paint the surrounding rocks. The lantern, undisturbed from its resting place beside the cave mouth, now cast a hellish red light on all the faithful as they spread out from their sanctuary.

"Alright!" Edward shouted in defiance of his terror. "He's here somewhere, but he's only one man!" He turned back to his people. "We are the faithful! We have been chosen by the Angel! Nothing can stop us!"

Spinning out of the surrounding darkness, whistling a low, inevitable dirge, a large, strange, L-shaped sword plunged itself into Edward MacAllister's chest.

Edward looked down, seeing shreds of his heart sticking out on the tip of the Angelic blade. Then he sighed and collapsed to his knees.

The faithful stood, frozen in shock, staring into the darkness. A roar shattered the silence and a pair of glowing amber eyes blazed to life, bathing the huddled mob in their demonic glow. The Beast leapt forward, charging straight at the cultists, bearing the monster wearing Adam Kadmon's face upon its back. As he passed Edward MacAllister, the hunter ripped his blade free, tearing the body apart with the violence of the action, sending a new shower of gore in all directions. Continuing the motion, the hunter swung his blades as the Beast roared into the scattering crowd of cultists, severing heads and limbs with equal ease and brutality. The attackers continued their charge through and past the crowd, to the side of the cave entrance, up an adjacent hill.

"Shoot!" someone desperately called. "Shoot!"

Dozens of gunshots, some single, others automatic, rang out. The gunfire was panicked, poorly aimed, and accomplished nothing except to unleash even more chaos. With their attackers no longer in sight, many of the cultists began firing in random directions, some high, some low, some even into the air, fearing that death might fall upon them from sky. The more frenzied the shots became, the more panicked the cultists became. Shouts became cries; cries became screams.

Within only a few seconds of the hunter's appearance, many of the cult members lost their courage and broke, fleeing in all directions. Because the random gunfire had not ceased, the sudden flight of many of the cultists caused an inevitable result. One after another of the cultists shot each other, many running directly into the path of their comrade's weapons. The renewed explosion of blood and gore only added to the terror and screams filling the air.

Above all the terror of the cult was the omnipresence of the hunter and his Beast. The shots and the screams were just a faint din when compared to the roar of the Beast. The sounds of the hunter's blades echoed everywhere, scraping along stone. The hills captured all sound, permitting no escape, so the cultists could not tell where their enemy was, only that he *was* there. The roar of the Beast was everywhere and the threat of the hunter's blades was everywhere.

Finally, the Beast appeared. Amber headlights flashed upon the cultists and, as one, they turned and fired. Bullets impotently bounced off mystical metal and flew over where a rider should have been. The motorcycle roared straight at them, bearing down on first one, then another screaming victim before turning in a wide arc to shower the terrified sinners in a cloud of stone shrapnel and dust.

Then the hunter leapt in among them from another direction. Blades flashed. The only people who screamed were those not yet slaughtered. The blades never stopped swirling in their flawless dance among the cultists. Shining death lashed out, severing heads and limbs, only to reverse themselves in a single, fluid motion so that the hunter could pummel face and body with his fists until nothing breathing remained. He destroyed every target with an efficiency that crossed into artistry.

The Beast joined in the slaughter with joyous abandon. Any cultist thinking himself fortunate to survive the hunter's blades suffered for that foolishness at the merciless fury of the Beast. Finally unleashed to vent all the frustration and rage at its suffering, the Beast chased down one cultist after another. The howls of dying fanatics mingled with a howling engine, the breaking of bones, and the rending of flesh. The Beast ground the wounded into the dirt, screams of pain finding equal response as did cries for mercy against the Beast's roar. Bullets fired at the machine bounced off with laughable ineffect, serving only to draw the monster's attention.

No enemy, no matter how courageous, could withstand so relentless, so brutal an assault. The cultists had little courage to begin with. The few remaining with any ability to fight fell, the rest scattered into the night, fleeing in all directions. Some of the fanatics retreated into the relative safety of the cave. The hunter left any remaining wounded to the Beast, his business being inside the cave. He whistled to the Beast, calling him off from his sport. "I'm going after the girl," he calmly said. "Guard the entrance. Make sure nobody comes in behind me."

The Beast revved his engine in agreement before continuing his joyous slaughter.

The hunter turned and entered the cave.

22

*A*pparently, the cave radiated courage. That was the hunter's assessment upon entering, at least. Very nearly the moment he stepped within the tunnels, the cultists had turned around and started attacking him again. Each corner held another fanatic, lunging forward to die. Each side chamber concealed another weapon-toting lunatic, eager for destruction.

A screaming fanatic lunged forward with a knife drawn. The hunter swept the weapon aside with his left blade and removed the attacker's head with the right. The distraction served though, as another one appeared to the hunter's side and lunged forward. He spun and blocked the outstretched gun just as it fired, reversing his right blade to drive his metal-reinforced fist into the newest attacker's face.

A scream from behind drew the hunter's attention. He glanced back in time to see yet another knife plunged into his back. The white leather coat held, of course, deflecting the worst of the attack, but the force of the impact was enough to drive the hunter to his knees. He pulled his fist free of the twitching body in front of him and drove the blade back into the last attacker. He then looked around, checking for more threats. Seeing none, he took several deep breaths to slow his heart and continued down.

The cavern complex was large. It sloped steadily downward, twisting constantly in different directions. Numerous small chambers and side-tunnels abounded, which would have provided the hunter with a problem in deciding where to go, had the cultists not set up a candlelit path.

The guns were something of a problem. With the number of automatic weapons these fanatics had at their disposal, they could have potentially stopped him. Fortunately, none of those remaining alive could shoot well and they lacked any coherent leadership. Additionally, they all had the habit of pulling the trigger and expending every bullet they had all at once.

"For her!" one screamed, giving the hunter all the warning he needed. He ducked back behind a wall as a hail of bullets raced past where his face had been only a moment before. In the instant the shots stopped, he darted out and rolled along the ground. The hunter came up in front of the shooter, batting his spent rifle aside and stabbing the cultist through the chest.

"For her!" another screamed from the left.

The hunter cursed and swung the body at the shooter, simultaneously rolling along the ground. A few of the bullets punched against his coat and brought growls of pain from his throat. The hunter kicked at the shooter and swung both blades, dividing the target into three pieces.

Fire exploded in the hunter's back to the sound of thunder. He stumbled but did not fall. Instead, the hunter turned and tried to take a step forward. A woman held a shotgun leveled, her eyes gleaming with insane devotion. "For her!" she almost moaned and fired again.

The hunter's vision filled with bright light and a great force sent him flying backwards.

The fanatic stepped forward, eyes wide and mouth agape. She held the shotgun ready, charging another round. The hunter lay still on the cavern floor. She took another step forward and nudged the body with the barrel of her weapon.

The hunter rolled, his shoulder forcing the barrel away as it fired. The sound was deafening and the heat infernal, but the shot missed. He kicked the woman's legs out from under her and reared up, roaring in fury and plunging a blade into her heart.

Seeing the immediate threat dealt with, the hunter stood and inspected himself. A dark black spot marred the white leather of his coat, and it felt as though someone had hit him in that spot with a tree trunk, but he could breathe, which meant his mission was not complete. He continued down.

Turning a corner, the hunter cursed and tried to step back. Too late. One of the cultists raised the end of a chemical sprayer and pointed it at the hunter. Attached to the end of the homemade weapon was a small fire source. The fanatic squeezed the trigger and the entire corridor filled with flame.

The hunter turned and ran, sheathing his blades, cursing himself for not wearing gloves as he beat at the flames that had wrapped around one sleeve. The coat itself suffered no damage, but the heat radiated to the unprotected portions of his body and his left hand was now greatly damaged. He ran away as more flames shot forth, bouncing into wall after wall as the flame-throwing cultist pursued. The hunter retreated until he had a few seconds and looked around, trying to locate one of the places of a previous ambush. Spotting what he needed and hearing the bursts of flame coming up from behind, the hunter dove into an adjoining cave.

The cultist with the flamethrower walked forward, hunting for the monster that had killed so many of her friends. At last, she spotted the hunter, kneeling in a dead-end cave. The fanatic was about to raise her weapon again when she spotted the weapon in her enemy's hands, a shotgun. The hunter fired.

A fireball erupted from the back of the fanatic, consuming her utterly before racing up and out of the cavern. The hunter stepped forward, dropping the shotgun and waving a hand in front of his face at the stench of charred flesh. He glanced at his left hand and grimaced, it was reddened and already showed signs of blistering. He still had full use for now, so the pain was irrelevant. In the distance, he heard chanting; the hunter drew his blades and followed the sound.

He reached a large, open cavern in which the last of the cultists had gathered. It was roughly circular, with a few odd stone protrusions scattered about. Six women had gathered around a rough altar of unhewn stone in the center of the chamber, their arms outstretched. The hunter recognized Hollman among them. It was they who were chanting. Candles were everywhere, creating a stifling heat and ominous glow, reminding the hunter of the Pit.

Holly was there, chained to the altar, continuing to struggle against her bonds. The cultists had gagged her. Her long hair had been bound back with a silken red cord, with matching red ribbons tied around her waist and thighs. They had stripped her of all other clothing, and covered her body in ritual markings of the First Language. Ironically, the markings that now covered the girl were an almost perfect replica of the hunter's own, except that where his had a list of many names, chronicling the innumerable successes of his long existence, only a single name marred Holly's young flesh, that of the Dark Angel.

While stretching against her bonds, Holly turned her head and saw the new arrival. Their gaze locked. Her eyes widened and tears appeared. Adam Kadmon looked down on her, seeing the humiliation to which she had been subjected. For the first time since receiving his unwanted soul, Adam Kadmon's rage overpowered the hunter's. A roar filled the cavern, echoing off the walls, a snarling declaration of destruction to everyone who had harmed Holly.

Four men dressed in the same robes as the women surrounding the altar turned at Adam's echoing battlecry. They raised police-issue batons and ran forward, climbing the natural stone steps that led up and out of the chamber. Adam did not wait for them. He leapt down the steps, swinging the blades. Two of the guards fell in pieces to his initial attack. A third swung his baton but Adam ducked the strike, reversing the blade on his right arm and driving that fist into the man's middle. He intercepted another desperate attack by the fourth guard and kicked him in the knee before delivering several rapid punches that sent the fourth guard falling down the stone steps. A quick swipe with one extended blade removed the third guard's head just as the man was beginning to recover. Adam then turned to the last of the cultists.

The final guard recovered his feet and was about to charge again. "Hold!" one of the women called out. "Join us."

The guard ran back into the circle of chanting women without hesitation.

Adam reached the floor of the chamber.

Elise MacAllister glared down imperiously at her enemy, as though he were nothing more than a minor inconvenience. "You are a fool to come here."

Adam took another step forward. His eyes were locked on the target ahead. His mind was clear of all thoughts save finally achieving his goals. He could see the resemblance between mother and daughter. The same hair, the same eyes. Elise was short, just as Holly was, and they had a similar, narrow build. There was even a similar look about the face. The hunter was not a creature that paid much attention to physical things, though. He looked beyond, at the soul. Elise was broken. She had suffered in her life and, rather than trying to heal, trying to accept the bad things that had happened to her and grow stronger because of them, she held on to all the bitterness and rage, letting it build within her until she found a way to take vengeance on the world.

"I know you, Za'afiel!" she declared.

The hunter flipped his blades back, behind his arms.

"When my children could not defeat you, I asked the Angel. You were revealed to me. Your threat to me and to my children was revealed to me. Continue the ceremony," she ordered to Hollman and the other women surrounding the altar.

The hunter continued forwards, destruction in his eyes.

The *Ímā* imperiously held up her hand. "Stop," she commanded.

He kept walking.

"You are a fool, Za'afiel," she said. "I know the ways of Celestials; the Angel has granted me power over them. You cannot stop my Lord from feasting upon this innocent."

Adam growled. The hunter's entire body tensed in anticipation before he leapt at the traitorous mother.

There was a flash of blinding light. The force of a thousand hammer-blows struck the hunter in the chest, sending him flying across the cavern to land in a heap of battered bones and bruised flesh.

"Do you see?" the *Ímā* gloated. "Do you see the power I have been granted? I am invincible through my Lord!"

Adam shook his head, grunting against the pain that coursed through his body. He gritted his teeth and stood, retrieving the blades. Turning back, the hunter narrowed his gaze and stared hard at the area surrounding the cultists. A thin ring of some dark fluid encircled the altar. He perceived the aura of power that radiated out of the circle, protecting them. It was feint, subtle, but present. It shimmered with a silent energy, clearly passive and designed specifically to prevent a Celestial from approaching.

"You can't hide in there forever," the hunter noted.

The *Ímā* laughed and stepped around the altar, staying within the ring that protected her. "You think I fear you, Za'afiel?" she demanded. The woman raised her hand and pointed a finger at the hunter. "I fear nothing so long as my Lord grants me his grace!"

A spear of pain thrust through the hunter's chest, lifting him off the ground and pinning him against the wall. Responding to the *Ímā*'s gestures, the hunter was dragged against the jagged cave wall, thrust up into the ceiling, and slammed into the floor. She clenched her fist and the spear of pain twisted in the hunter's chest causing him to writhe in agony.

"I am all powerful here," the *Ímā* declared. "My Angel has given me power over all the Celestials." She continued to form different gestures, changing the nature of the hunter's pain. "The Angel has taught me much," she said with a worshipful smile. "When I was told of you, I asked, 'How do I create a barrier through which even mighty Za'afiel cannot pass?' That circle, like the one into which we will summon the Angel himself, is made of a holy concoction." She held up her arm, letting the sleeve of her robe fall. A fresh red line ran the length of her forearm. "I, and each of my daughters, gave freely of our blood to create the circle. It empowers me; it empowers me over you, Fallen One!"

The hunter snarled.

The *Ímā* laughed. "Yes, I know you. The Angel told me your Name. You cannot stop us, for you cannot reach us!" She let her hand fall, allowing the pain to momentarily end. Turning away from the hunter, she held out her hand to one of the other cultists. "I will not destroy you, though I have been given the power. You will be allowed to witness my ascension."

Hollman lifted a curved knife. "We are ready, my *Ímā*."

The *Ímā* turned back to her daughter and took up the knife.

"There's something important you should know," the hunter gasped.

Elise did not bother turning, but instead raised the knife above Holly's heart. "And what would that be?"

Adam Kadmon threw aside his blades, the last vestiges of what he once was. He completed the act begun months ago, shedding himself of his past life, his past power, his past self. This was an act available to any Celestial, though only a handful ever did. The pain was horrific, beyond anything an enemy or friend could ever inflict. Everything that was the hunter, that was powerful and relentless and eternal, boiled away in a single shattering instant. The great Celestial power that had condemned Angels, slaughtered armies, leveled cities, and sundered empires melted away. In its place was a soul, a single spark of hope and fear, of love and hate, and Free Will. The hunter was no more, leaving only Adam Kadmon.

There was a flurry of movement as Adam charged forward, leaping across the barrier without resistance. The lone remaining guard, caught unawares, tried to intercept him, but was knocked aside for his trouble. Two of the women ran forward. Adam grabbed the outstretched arm of one, wrenching it in a circle that forced its owner to flip in the air, tumbling away from the altar. An instant later, he spun, driving his fist into the back of her skull. When she tried to turn, Adam ducked under the wild swing of her arm, wrapped his hand around the back of her neck, and, pulling her down into the strike, drove his knee into her middle. He then threw her down to join her comrade.

By now, the last of the guards had recovered and charged toward Adam, screaming in desperate fury. The baton was easily taken away and, with a low swing, used to dislocate the young man's knee. A final strike to the side of the skull removed the guard from the battle.

Adam turned to the *Ímā* and her final two cultists. A screaming woman leapt onto his back. He dropped to one knee, reaching behind and pulling forward the head his hands found. The woman came flipping over Adam's shoulder to land at in front of him. Adam stood quickly and drove his boot into the target's face with enough force to cave it in.

The *Ímā* kept gesturing angrily at Adam.

He shook his head. "Your Angel forgot to mention the drawback to your little tricks."

She looked to her hands. "I need *more!*" she snarled. She glanced at the woman standing beside her and, lifting the knife she still held, plunged it into her follower's chest. "You die for *me!*" she screamed.

Hollman gasped at this and backed away. Her eyes went from Elise to Adam. Her decision made, the woman turned and fled down a nearby tunnel.

The *Ímā* ripped the knife out of her follower's chest and rubbed her free hand along the wound, bathing it in fresh blood. She then made to turn back to her enemy.

From behind her, before Elise could turn, Adam was at her back. He grabbed the *Ímā* from behind and slammed her head into the altar. Stumbling back, she dropped the knife, which Adam caught before it could hit the ground. In one fluid movement, he snatched the blade that Elise had planned to use on her own daughter and drove it into the woman's abdomen. Snarling into her ear, Adam said, "Your power only works on Celestials!" He ripped the blade out and let it fall to the ground, stepping away.

Elise stood for a moment, frozen with her hand over the mortal wound to her abdomen, a newest tear over an old scar. She looked into her daughter's eyes, seeking something, perhaps comfort, perhaps forgiveness, but finding nothing. Holly saw only the monster that had been ready to murder her.

Adam turned back to the altar as Elise fell. It took only a moment to discern the simple latches that had secured Holly's bonds and release them, freeing her from the chains and gag. He wordlessly draped his white leather coat around her small shoulders. As small as she was, the large garment was more than enough to cover her nakedness.

They stood there for a moment, facing each other, in the ruins of the cult's holy site.

"Sorry it took me so long."

"Yeah, well… fashionably late, but still a big entrance." Tears stood in the girl's eyes. Her entire body shook with the need to release them but still she fought.

"You want to get the Hell out of here?"

She nodded. "Yeah," she said through a choked sob. "Uh… this place is kind of played out."

They turned and started walking away but paused when the *Imä*'s voice called out. "Angel of Destruction!" she weakly cried.

Adam froze. He held Holly turned away but glanced back himself. Elise had climbed onto the altar, taking her daughter's place. She lay with her head turned towards them. "You saved her life," the woman said through gasps of dying breath. "But… I… still…. win…"

"Shit!" Too late, he took a step to stop the fanatic.

Elise plunged the knife into her own breast.

"Holly," Adam said in a very calm voice. "I need you to listen to me very carefully." He held her shoulders in a firm grasp. She was turned away from the altar and would remain that way if he had any control.

"Ok," she replied in a small voice.

"I need you to kneel down and close your eyes. I need you to cover your ears and start singing a song. I need you to sing a song that makes you happy, the happiest song you know. Sing it over and over until I come back and tell you to stop. Don't stop singing, don't open your eyes. Don't turn around. Do you understand?"

"Where are you going?"

"Holly, I need you to start singing right now."

She nodded and obeyed. Kneeling as a child would in church, Holly knelt on the cave floor with Adam's white coat spread around her and, with her small hands covering her tiny ears, and she sang a soft lullaby, a warm reminder of loving family.

Seeing this done, Adam turned and resolutely faced the Dark Angel. He had skin the color of black marble. A burning crown of gold encircled his long, perfectly white hair. His two pairs of grey wings were both folded back in calm rest as his twin eyes of burning blood stared directly at Adam.

"I know you, Paimon," Adam said in a voice that did not betray the dread that now filled his unwanted soul. Even before, as an Angel himself, Adam would have had doubt in this confrontation. To face a Dominion was no slight thing, especially one who had rebelled against God. "You don't belong here."

Paimon glanced down at the dying woman who had summoned him, and then back at Adam.

"Your bargain was with these humans. They're all dead. Your bargain is done. I call on you to leave this place peacefully."

Paimon said nothing, but merely raised an eyebrow, cocking his head to the side. The implication was clear.

"We both know I can't make you," Adam admitted. "I won't waste our time with idle threats. You have nothing further to gain here. Your worshippers are all dead."

"Not all," the Dark Angel whispered.

Adam was driven to his knees at the sound of the Dominion's voice. Breathing heavily, he put a hand to his ear and came away with blood. Looking back up at the Dark Angel, Adam tried again. "Most are dead. The rest have fled. Their spirit is broken, their leader is slain."

"Pacts were made," Paimon whispered.

Again, Adam's mind flared with agony. Blood spurted from his mouth. He fought to keep his control in the face of such punishment and somehow keep from being overwhelmed. "You kept your end of the bargain, but there has been too much treachery on this end. Look around you."

The Dark Angel glanced around.

"You are trapped by your own wisdom. You told the cult how to trap an Angel and they did. They trapped you. The time of the bargain has come, and you are trapped."

Paimon frowned.

"You cannot escape until the dawn. You can kill me now, but that gains you nothing; I was not the one who trapped you. You can pursue those who cheated you, but that also gains you nothing. Now you know that those in this area who would make a pact with you seek only to cheat you. You need not expend any energy in seeking out those who cheated you. They became dependent on your information and many will seek you out again. When they call on you, you will be ready for their trap and can destroy them. If they never call on you, then your gifts to them are useless anyway."

The Dark Dominion considered Adam's suggestion. Finally, he nodded. Adam began backing away. "One exception." This time, Adam was able to stay on his feet, though just barely, a tear of blood running down his face.

"Yes?"

Paimon glanced down at the dead woman and ran a light hand along her body. He casually opened her robe, pushing it aside, and touched the wound that was, at that moment, claiming her life. The Dark Dominion casually ripped free the knife and wiped away the wound, both the new one, and the old. With a gasp, Elise's eyes opened. The woman blinked in confusion until she saw the Dark Angel standing above her.

"You will pay the debt," he whispered.

Adam turned away, grabbing Holly but motioning for her to keep singing. He silently wished that he could also cover his ears and sing, the better to drown out the agonized screams coming from behind them. He held Holly tightly as he guided his charge up and away from that evil place, sparing a brief glance towards where his blades lay. They still called to him, shining in the darkness, a bright memory of his past. Adam continued on, leading Holly out of the cave, away from its offensive shadows.

At the cave entrance, the Beast was loudly revving his engine. A strong wind had picked up, carrying with it the scent of rain and the rumble of distant thunder. All the noise made it almost impossible to notice the screams that continued to echo up from below. Almost. Adam knew, as the Beast knew, those screams would continue until the dawn forced the Dark Angel's retreat. Of course, Elise MacAllister would die in the instant before the Dark Dominion was forced to retreat. Then, with Judgement, the woman's suffering would begin in earnest.

"So, what happens now?" Holly asked, having to yell over the Beast's revving engine.

Adam climbed onto the waiting motorcycle. "We ride off into the sunset."

Holly looked around at the darkness. "I don't think we're going to have one of those for a while yet."

"Figure of speech." He reached for the handles but flinched when his left hand made contact. The burns on his hand throbbed.

Holly stepped forward and took his hand. "Fall again?"

"Once was enough."

She reached down and removed one of the ribbons tied around her thigh, wrapping it around his burned hand.

"I doubt that's sanitary," Adam noted.

"You're right. Your hand is filthy."

Turning away, he tried very hard to keep the smile from his face. He failed.

Holly looked at him with a slight smile. "You should try doing that more often."

"When I have reason."

"Really though," Holly continued. "What happens now?"

"For now, you stay with me. Take some time to figure things out. When you're ready, you move on to whatever you want."

Holly thought about it. "That might take a little while. I didn't really have a clue before all this shit happened."

Adam shrugged. "I'm not going anywhere." He jabbed a thumb to the passenger seat.

She climbed on, arranging the white leather coat so that it would not fly up during their ride, exposing her lack of clothes underneath. "One question."

"You mean one more?" he corrected.

"Ok, one more."

"Shoot."

"Why'd she call you the Angel of Destruction?"

Adam sighed. "I guess if you're going to be hanging around me, there's a few things you should know."

"Like what?" Holly asked, wrapping her arms around Adam.

He hit the Beast's clutch. "For starters, before I Fell, my name was Za'afiel. I was one of God's Angels of Destruction."

23

"So what happened with the bomb threat?" Adam asked.

Isandro finished off his coffee and signaled to the waitress for another. "Well, thanks to the slow response at Agarés, not to mention all of their security procedures for getting access to all the sensitive areas, it took until dawn to finish sweeping their buildings." They had met late in the morning at the café across from the Police headquarters. Neither man had slept, but had felt the need to complete the whole sorry affair before finding the rest they had earned.

Adam swallowed another bite of his breakfast, struggling a bit with the heavy bandages over his left hand. "Sounds like a long night."

The good cop nodded. "I can't count the number of times the lieutenant wanted to pack it in, but Aubrey kept threatening to have his job, so we stayed."

"I bet he was pissed when you never found anything."

"Would you believe we actually found a bomb?"

"You're kidding."

"Nope," Isandro chuckled. "It was some shitty pipe-job thrown in a dumpster that probably never would have gone off, but yeah, we found one."

"Well, I guess you never know what you'll find until you look."

"So how did last night go?"

"Saved the girl, killed the bad guys, won the day."

Isandro lifted his cup. "Let's hear it for the good guys."

Adam raised his own glass of orange juice and then drank deeply. "So, what's the girl going to do now?"

"We figure it's a good idea if she lays low for a while," Adam replied. "There's still a lot of those cultists out there. Besides the ones who ran off, there's still the ones with the cops and on the base who were called away. One of them might get an idea."

"So she'll stay with you?" Isandro asked with a side glance.

"It's not like that."

"Sure, sure."

"Hey, kiss my sore ass, alright."

"Yeah, I'll bet it's sore."

Aubrey signed off on the last of the paperwork for the morning and handed it off to her new assistant. With a moment alone to think, the executive turned in her seat to look out the window. The view was, as always, pleasant. Disanté was an attractive town when viewed from above. The minimal pollution was masked by the rolling hills and bright sunlight. The organized grid of streets and buildings gave a welcome sense of organization. All in all, Aubrey could normally look out her office windows and feel a sense of peace in her otherwise hectic life.

She should be feeling calm, after all. Her commitment to the Dark Angel was removed. She had gained all the information she needed from the creature, and had needed to give little, almost nothing, in return. It would not be coming after her, nor interfering in any of her upcoming plans. The cult that had been a growing thorn in her side, and an annoying distraction for her subordinates, was removed. Most importantly, Aubrey had a new... asset available.

He had called not long after dawn. The conversation had been brief. He had not bothered to thank her for providing the false documentation that had granted him access to Fort Burleson, and Aubrey would have thought less of him if he had. He had not given her any unneeded details of the evening, nor bothered discussing the fate of Miss MacAllister. Like a good agent, he had told her only what she needed to know and cared about hearing.

"The cult leadership is dead," he had said. "Most of the members are still alive, but they're scattered. Your old assistant was one of the ones who ran. My interest in her is done, so if you want her, she's all yours. The cult could still reform, but I've made an arrangement with your Dark Angel that, if they try to contact him again, he'll wipe them out. That goes for you, as well. He won't come after you, as long as you don't try to contact him again. Your bargain is over."

Hollman's survival was irritating, but incidental. Any knowledge she had was not so sensitive that it could not be safeguarded against. Any damage she could do would be incidental, at worst. Hunting her down would be more in the nature of setting an example. Necessary but hardly critical. Aubrey viewed the project as more of an entertaining distraction than a chore; it would be amusing to see how long Hollman could elude her and what end would eventually befall the traitor. Perhaps Aubrey could even convince Mr. Kadmon to join in the hunt.

His voice had deepened then, growling and powerful. "I'll be watching you from now on Aubrey," he had said to her.

Impudent bastard.

"I'm going to be paying much closer attention, so that this kind of thing doesn't happen again. If you get out of line, I'll be paying you another visit." And then he had hung up.

"Um… Ms. Aubrey?" Her assist had returned without announcing her presence or requesting permission.

Aubrey opened her eyes with a start, not remembering having closed them. The executive also did not remember at what point she had slipped one hand around her own throat and the other into her business skirt.

Lust turned to rage, and Aubrey grabbed a lamp on her desk and hurled it at the intrusive assistant, striking the fool on the temple. "GET OUT!!!!" she screeched.

Although stunned by the blow, Aubrey's assistant retreated, bleeding from the wound.

Aubrey sat at her desk, seething in fury at her own weakness.

Damn him! DAMN HIM!!! How dare he!?!

Adam entered the Waystation, wondering how his life had become so complicated. Candice was, as usual, behind the bar. She had noted his approach but pretended to give him no notice.

Oh good, we're doing this now.

"Uh… hey," he said, sitting down at his usual spot.

She continued cleaning glasses. "Hey yourself."

"So… about yesterday."

Insane cultists would be great, right about now.

"Yeah?"

"Yeah. You see, I'm… well, my life is… well, it's complicated. I've got… issues."

"I'll say."

Adam let out a breath explosively. "Well, the thing is… since I got here, you've been the only person that hasn't… I don't… that hasn't pissed me off."

Candice stopped and stood there, looking at him. "Well, thank you."

"Well that's really saying something," he hastily added. "Because, you know, *everyone* pisses me off."

"Uh huh."

"And it's just that… well… I'm kind of a scum bag but I don't want to do anything that… well, if I did anything to hurt you... your feelings that is…" Adam just stopped talking at that point. He thought it was the most intelligent thing he could do.

"Wow," Candice remarked. The bartender shook her head and grabbed a glass, pouring the man some water. "You really suck at this."

He could only nod.

"Here you are, runnin' around town, kickin' ass in the name of savin' a little girl." She continued at her minor work. "And yet, when the time comes you have to talk to a woman about feelin's, you might as well be at the back of the short bus on the way to the fair."

"I don't know if I'd go *that* far."

"Oh, I would," Candice replied. "Hon, you're damaged, I get it." She leaned over in front of him, stirring his drink with her finger. "But I got news for you, we're *all* damaged. You might have had a few more trips on the psycho tilt-a-whirl than most, but you're also a lot more stand-up than most." She licked her finger. "You were hurt, and I felt really bad for you because you were hurtin'. Get over yourself. If the day ever comes when I do decide to take you for a spin, you'd best just hold on and pray."

Adam blinked and could only stare with wide eyes as Candice picked up some boxes and carried them into the back. "Huh."

"Well, that was sweet," a voice said from the door.

Adam shook his head and sighed. "I was hoping you'd leave," he grumbled.

Simkiel moved next to Adam and took the adjoining stool. "Why would I do that?"

Adam took a drink before answering. "Because you finished manipulating me into bringing the girl into my life." He raised the glass. "Fine, I did it. The girl's been saved, I'm embracing humanity. Now fuck off."

Simkiel smiled. "You're making an awful lot of assumptions, old friend. First, I wasn't the one who got you to take up the girl's cause, you barmaid was. Second, at no point did I ever even suggest that you have the girl stay with you. And third, what makes you think she isn't in danger anymore?"

Adam looked hard at the Angel.

Simkiel shrugged. "You said it to your cop friend earlier. The cult is still out there, licking its wounds. Paimon is still out there, and he was promised her flesh. You know how he is. I'd say she's anything but out of danger. And then there's her association with you."

Adam said nothing.

"Thousands of years as an Angel of Destruction," Simkiel mused. "I can't imagine how many enemies you've made. All those... well let's call them people... that have been positively salivating for a chance at vengeance on any Celestial, let alone an Angel of Destruction. Now here you are, Adam Kadmon, one of the Fallen. And you have a sidekick." The Angel glanced sidelong at Adam. "I imagine once word gets out that you're here, things will get very... interesting."

"Would there be any reason to think that you, or anyone else, would be making sure those... *people* hear about me?"

Simkiel laughed. "You really are a fool. I don't have to do anything. You've been here two months, and you've already started kicking up every anthill in the area." The Angel narrowed his eyes. "In very short order, dear brother, near you is going to be a very dangerous place to be."

Adam stood. "I don't care about your threats, Simkiel. I don't care about your manipulations and I don't care about you. The whole Chorus can go screw itself, just like they told me to." He started to leave.

"That's not exactly the way I remember your trial."

"Just stay out of my way, Simkiel. You and all your kind."

"We were once your kind to," the Angel reminded him. "We'll be seeing you, Za'afiel."

Adam paused at the door. Glancing back, he said, "That's not my name anymore." Then he left.

Simkiel turned back to face the bar. "No," he agreed, "it isn't. I wonder who you'll be now."

24

Days passed. Then weeks. Summer continued. Holly withdrew into herself. Adam tried to help her as best he could but knew nothing about how to deal with her type of circumstances. What does someone say to a girl whose parents tried to sacrifice her to torturous rape and death? He weathered the storms of weeping as best he could, offering what support he could. He got the movies and food she requested. He said nothing when she claimed his bedroom and remade it in her image. He rearranged the apartment according to her commands. Other than that, he watched helplessly, waiting for some sign as to what he was supposed to do.

One day, Holly became a blur of activity. She used the computer she insisted he buy to make strange arrangements. She used money he provided to buy things but would not tell him what. Finally, after a week of preparation, Holly declared a grand unveiling.

"What the Hell am I looking at?"

"It's our new office!" she replied cheerfully, grandly gesturing at the empty office space.

Standing in the mostly deserted parking lot, Adam was trying very hard not to swear. They were not quite in the middle of nowhere. More like nowhere-adjacent. The business center, as Holly had called it, consisted of a half dozen spaces, of which only two were occupied. One had an Asian massage parlor, and the other had a sign offering to buy old gold and jewelry.

Now the third had an ex-Angel of Destruction and his spunky sidekick.

"Office," Adam finally said. "Why?"

She took his arm and happily led him inside. "Just come and see!" she gushed.

The inside was, if possible, even less inspiring. There was little furniture, only a few chairs and an old folding table with a hole in it. Several ceiling tiles were missing, and something was watching them from the exposed roof. The floor was not carpeted, unless one counted those areas with mysterious fluids. "Oh, now I see. It's all so clear."

"Don't be an ass," she chided him. Holly walked to the center of the main area, that section not walled off by pieces of wall, and turned in a slow circle with her arms outstretched. "Use your imagination."

"Alright. I'm imagining *not* throwing you in the river."

"Oh my God, you're so hilarious," she replied in an even voice.

"Holly, what the Hell do we need with an office?" A rat ran across the floor. "Other than to hunt for dinner?"

She skipped over to the table, upon which a small box rested. Opening the box, Holly pulled out a small card and brought it over to Adam. "We need it for this," she said, presenting the card to him.

"Sentinel Consultations," he read. "We investigate, we protect, we believe." He shook his head slightly in confusion but then paused as understanding set in. "No," he told her firmly.

"Why not?"

"It's bad enough I got dragged into your mess," he grumbled. "And look what that got me." He began counting items off on the fingers of a severely burned hand that he now could barely use. "I got beaten. I got shot at. I was in a car wreck." He held up his bandaged hand. "I got set on *fire*. I had to face a damned Dark Angel. I had to make a deal with that damned Aubrey. I'm pretty sure I've got a price on my damned head. And, oh yeah, I got *you*."

"Exactly," she beamed. "You got me. See all the good that can come out of helping people?"

"Wait, what?"

Holly crossed her arms over her chest. "Before we met, you were doing nothing but drinking yourself to death. Now you're out and active and happy."

"Well out and active," he muttered.

"People need someone they can count on," she continued, ignoring his grumpiness. "The cops here can't help or don't care. The government is only interested in helping themselves. Who does that leave? You told me the other day that when you stopped being an Angel, you lost your purpose." She held out her hands. "*This* can be your purpose."

"But I hate people," Adam countered. "People are stupid. All this will be is people coming in, whining about problems they got themselves into. Because. They. Are. Stupid."

"A lot of it will be that," Holly conceded. "But there will also be people who genuinely just need help. People who deserve a chance."

He just growled and shook his head. "No."

"Yes," she argued.

"No," he snapped.

She grabbed the front of his coat. "Yyyeeessssss."

He put a finger in her face. "No."

She looked at him through her big, round eyes and pouted out her lower lip. "Yes?" she said in a tiny voice.

He put his fists on his hips. "No," he countered.

The front door opened, and a woman entered. She wore expensive clothes and was very neat, but she moved very hesitantly. Her makeup and hair were done with obvious care, as was the attention taken to conceal a black eye. "Excuse me?" she said timidly. She glanced down at a business card. "Is this, 'Sentinel Consultations'?"

"No!" Adam barked.

Holly punched him in the stomach and then ducked around his shoulder. "Yes," she said, moving to the woman.

"What? No!"

"Is there something wrong?" the woman asked, looking at Adam in concern.

"Oh, don't mind him," Holly said, putting her arm around the woman. "He hasn't had his coffee yet."

"But it's three-thirty."

"I know, right? You see how grumpy he is. Is there something we can help you with?"

"Well, I'm not sure," she looked around the office.

Without missing a step, Holly said, "You'll have to excuse the mess, we just today moved into this building. Can you imagine how I felt when I walked in?" She pointed a thumb at Adam. "*That one* got this place. He thought it was just fine."

The woman could not help but smile.

"I'd like to offer you something, but maybe you'd just like to talk?" Holly suggested.

The woman nodded and tears formed in her eyes. "It's… it's my husband. He…"

Holly led her over to the two chairs and sat her down. The woman began sobbingly relating a story of abuse from her husband. It was a problem, Adam had no doubt, he would soon be forced to deal with. A problem that would lead to him being beaten and shot at. It was likely a problem of her own creation. Holly nodded in sympathy, uncaring towards Adam's feelings. In a moment of precognition, he foresaw a whole series of people, each one more annoying than the last, crying their own miseries to the girl, and her insisting that each was deserving of "their" help.

Adam let out a deep breath explosively as he surrendered. He stepped outside and walked to the far end of the parking lot. Raising his fists to Heaven, knowing to whom blame rested for the Hell he must now endure, Adam Kadmon accepted his life.

"Damn. Damn! DAMN!!!"

Amen

Adam and Holly
continue their adventures in
Fallen Justice

ABOUT THE AUTHOR

William Price Jr is a teacher of writing and literature. A veteran of two wars, he turned to storytelling to either maintain his sanity, or finish it off properly.